G000054123

The Unknown Stigma

1

〈The Mystery〉

HS PRESS

Copyright © 2022 by Ryuho Okawa
English translation © Happy Science 2022
Original title: *Shousetsu Jujika no Onna 1 <Shinpi hen>*
HS Press is an imprint of IRH Press Co., Ltd.
Tokyo
ISBN 13: 979-8-88737-013-2

The Unknown Stigma

1

〈The Mystery〉

Ryuho Okawa

HS PRESS

1.

It has been over a month since Junichi Yamasaki of the Metropolitan Police Department's First Criminal Investigation Division heard the rumor.

The rumor goes that the incident broke out at Arisugawa Park in Hiroo.

In early summer, around dusk, when all was quiet, a loud scream of a young female suddenly echoed throughout the wooded park.

Three people from the neighborhood heard the cry and rushed toward the sound, but by the time they arrived, the female victim was gone. In her place was a sturdy man, knocked out on the ground with his eyes rolled back and foaming at the mouth. The man had loosened his belt and started to take off his pants, so it seemed obvious that the man had intended to assault the woman. In fact, evidence left on the man's clothes suggested that he was just about to *do* it.

The dead body was turned over to the Identification Division. It was initially thought that a woman was attacked, but the dead body was actually that of a man. He turned out to be a U.S. Marine on his way to roam around Roppongi.

Even Yamasaki's detective instinct did not tell him anything.

Could there be a Japanese woman who can kill a U.S. Marine—granted, it could be self-defense—or at least cause a man to die from shock and escape on her end? Even if she has a high rank in karate or aikido, the woman would not be able to resist for more than five minutes if a Marine mounted her and choked her. But the woman was gone by the time the two men and a woman from a nearby crossroad rushed to the site of the shrieking cry. It all happened in a matter of two or three minutes. A 6′7″ man was helplessly dead. There was no sign of a knife wound, nor was there a bullet, a nunchaku, or a rope at the crime scene. The man was not even bleeding. Was he electrocuted? But that can't be. An on-site investigation was conducted, and a female police officer acted out the scenario; she defended against a male police officer with a fifth-degree black belt in judo, but they concluded that it was impossible.

At the site, there was an imprint of a woman pushed against the ground and a single button that must have been ripped off from the chest of her blouse when she fought the man.

If only the body was bleeding from a stab wound or something, Yamasaki thought.

He rather intensely thought of different scenarios because he didn't want to turn this into a diplomatic issue, but there was too little evidence to solve the mystery.

That night, Yamasaki dreamed he was flying. He was about to fly across from the Hiroo crossroad to the sky right above the park. He saw the dark, wooded area below. *That's right*, he thought to himself. The crime happened around that empty spot surrounded by *ume* plum trees. What kind of a Japanese woman, while being pushed down by a Marine, could instantaneously kill the man without leaving a single bruise or wound—without rupturing his internal organs—and seemingly escape so easily? Perhaps she was a psychic with spiritual powers. If so, this case would be challenging even for the police.

After some time, however, a similar incident occurred in Odaiba.

An athlete on a run by the seashore seemed to have been heading toward the gun battery monument that stood in Daiba Park. Similar to the previous incident, the athlete was found flat on his back and foaming at the mouth. Just like the Marine, the athlete's dead body was simply lying there, completely unscathed.

The suspect was just one person, and it was evident they did not use a weapon. Poison was not used either. The person must have somehow knocked out the large man with a single blow and nonchalantly walked away toward the cinema complex in Odaiba.

This jogging athlete was also found to have had his urethra full of semen, which suggested that he was assaulting a woman.

Were these cases indicative of a serial killing, or were they coincidental and isolated accidents? The two incidents could have been caused by a male criminal disguised as a female; this could not be ruled out. In modern times, it is not always possible to determine a person's gender based on appearance alone.

If that were true, the culprit might be a perverted man, somewhat resembling the Grim Reaper—dressing like a female, luring the victim to attack him, and finishing him off. If Bruce Lee in his glory days was gazing at the ocean while dressed like a female and was attacked by a foolish athlete from the rear, he could have instantaneously finished him off.

Even so, although the "how" could be reasonably speculated, Yamasaki still couldn't answer the "why." He would have a clue for identifying and finding the culprit if, say, the culprit's parents were killed or their romantic partner was injured, but there was evidently no motive of that sort. Could it have been the work of an alien? How foolish. Even if the time he was living in did not exclude the influence of aliens as a possibility, Yamasaki knew that it was not a thought a respectable detective should be having. Yamasaki, who had the highest intelligence quotient (IQ) within the First Criminal Investigation Division, put his brain into high gear.

2.

The whole picture of the case was still ambiguous, and Yamasaki didn't have any definite convictions. The case was still too early in processing to hold a general meeting with the Metropolitan Police Department's First Criminal Investigation Division, so he decided to begin a secret investigation with just three people, including Doman Yogiashi (age 27) and female detective Yuri Okada (age 25) with Junichi Yamasaki (age 30) himself as chief. Doman Yogiashi, as his name suggests, was a self-proclaimed descendant of an *onmyoji*, a yin-yang master who has supernatural powers, named Doman Ashiya from the Heian period. Yamasaki, however, was not sure about the truth of his claim.

Doman was a clever man who graduated from Kyoto University's Department of Religion. After graduation, he took up an offer from a technology venture firm, which went bankrupt two years later.

He had no choice but to look for another workplace, and when he searched for a job that leveraged his third-degree black belt skill in karate, the police force took a liking to him. In those days, there had been an influx of incidents caused by malicious religious groups as well as many IT-related scams, so the higher-ups decided that they would recruit detectives who were also somewhat peculiar themselves.

Yuri Okada was a bilingual who spent her junior and senior high school days in New York because her father, a banker, was assigned there. She later enrolled in the Tokyo University of Foreign Studies, but the classes there were so mundane that she found herself immersed in mystery novels. She's a so-called nerd with her ability to list out, in three minutes, 100 different ways to kill a person.

The recent cases started with the death of a U.S. Marine, so the "victim," or the criminal, was suspected to be a foreigner. If the criminal was a professional of planned murder, Yuri's mystery-nerd brain could come in handy. Yamasaki also covertly maintained the idea that Yuri could be used as bait if circumstances called for it. He even considered bleaching Yuri's hair blonde if the almost-assaulted woman was a foreigner. It was also possible that the female victim might have had a male partner in crime; while she lured the man into assaulting her, the male partner could have approached the man from behind and stabbed him with a sharp needle, like a professional killer depicted in a popular Japanese historical TV show. In this case, Yuri's tall and slender figure might come in handy to get men to think she is a foreigner.

Speaking of ways to kill someone, Yamasaki repeatedly watched a DVD of a historical movie, *The Death Blade: Ogre's Claw*, to study different methods of murder. In the movie, a sword expert uses the secret art of "The Death Blade: Ogre's Claw" to kill his corrupt superior in the castle. Just as the sword expert passes the target in the hallway, he stabs his superior's heart with a needle-like small knife hidden in his palm. The chief retainer, dressed in *kamishimo*, a traditional Japanese ceremonial dress, suddenly falls to the ground without a single knife wound. Even if the doctor examines the corpse, the conclusion is this: "It was probably a heart attack." It remains a mystery how the sword expert knocked his superior out without visibly shedding blood or using a sword.

Yamasaki went to a ramen noodle shop he frequently ate at with Yuri Okada and asked her a question as a quick brain exercise: "Is there a good way to kill a nasty boss as you pass him in the hallway without giving yourself away?"

"Invisibility cloak," said Yuri. "Become invisible." "Invite him to tea and make him drink poison that kicks in one hour later." "Provoke the man into assaulting you, and while acting as though you're a victim, tape his nose and mouth and suffocate him." "Hmm, maybe another one is to pierce his chest with a long needle, like a professional killer." She continued. "Other than that, you can use black magic and curse him to death. Doman is a specialist in this field." As expected, Yuri was quick on her feet.

Junichi Yamasaki himself was called a prodigy during his elementary school days, and all went well for him up until he entered the Junior and Senior High Schools at Komaba affiliated with University of Tsukuba—known to be Japan's number one feeder school to the University of Tokyo. Once he entered, however, his grades plummeted, and he couldn't get into the University of Tokyo, Waseda University, or Keio University. After spending an extra year preparing for the next entrance exam, he passed it and went on to the University of Tsukuba. Even though the Senior High School at Komaba is an affiliated school, Yamasaki was the only one in his grade to have entered the University of Tsukuba. Things such as a sense of patriotism, loyalty, and commitment to a company as well as school spirit had been wiped out of Japan. If he had entered the University of Tokyo, Faculty of Law, from the Senior High School at Komaba, becoming a superintendent general or the commissioner general of the National Police Agency would not have only been a dream for him. But now, he was satisfied if he could get an average promotion as a public servant. To begin with, Yamasaki had failed his college entrance exam and had to spend an extra year studying because he had practiced kendo with excessive diligence during junior and senior high school. In his last year of senior high, Yamasaki thought his friends would be proud when he got his third-degree in kendo. Instead, they said, "Now you're failing for sure. You'll be delayed a year. You're bound to be rejected by Sundai Preparatory School, and you're off to a second-rate school." His friends got together and held what they called a

Sure-to-Fail Party at a karaoke lounge, where they made Yamasaki sing a song called "Separation at Age 22" by the singer group Kaguya-hime, not just once but three times.

His friends' predictions were spot-on. As the only student to have entered the University of Tsukuba, he was frustrated to see his friends become politicians and bureaucrats. *Hmph, I'll arrest them*, he thought, and that's how he decided to join the police force and become a detective. This was the only way for him to take advantage of the third-degree skill in kendo, which he obtained by not attending cram school. Even so, whenever he was drunk, he regretfully complained about how he failed to become a superintendent general.

Every so often, his bosses or colleagues would call out to him with sarcasm, "Oh! There goes Superintendent General Yamasaki!" But Yamasaki always thought, "They're foolish to make fun of me. What's inside my head easily competes with that of a Superintendent General."

Just then, Doman Yogiashi rushed into the ramen shop.

"Chief, there was a third murder."

"Location?" Yamasaki asked.

"It's Yoyogi Park."

"Victim?"

"He's apparently flat on his back and foaming at the mouth, eyes rolled back, dead, and grasping a cut end of a bra."

Yuri Okada chimed in. "The bra finally came up. Now we can think of these deaths as a case of a serial murder related to sex crimes, right?"

Chief Yamasaki gulped. "Alright, we're heading out."

Of course, the three of them were going to the crime site: Yoyogi Park.

3.

Now, here is a little more information on Yuri Okada.

Intelligence is not enough for a person to become a police officer. Since her junior and senior high school days in New York, Yuri has been learning Kyokushin Karate for over 10 years. She grew up hearing many legendary stories about its founder, Masutatsu Oyama, from her father. Yuri went to a dojo that one of Oyama's leading disciples opened, and there she heard great stories too. Kyokushin Karate is full-contact karate, unlike traditional karate that avoids direct hits. The practice often comes with many injuries, but those who practice it are said to be exceptionally stronger than those who practice traditional karate or judo. The legendary master Masutatsu Oyama is said to have cut off the thin neck of a beer bottle with his karate chop and folded a 10-yen coin in half with just his thumb and index finger. The legendary figure is also said to have defeated many giant wrestlers in America, and he is known for having thrown a buffalo onto the ground by grabbing its horns.

One day, to test how powerful Kyokushin Karate really is, Willie Williams, a Black fighter with a third-degree black belt, went up against a human-eating bear.

Williams had a bit of an advantage because the bear was gagged and surrounded by several members of the Hunters Association carrying tranquilizer guns. When the bear stood up, however, it was almost 10 feet tall, and it weighed several hundred pounds; so there was a chance Williams could lose his life if he received a punch from left or right or if the bear stormed into him headfirst.

The result was outstanding. The third-degree black belt holder of Kyokushin Karate kicked and killed the human-eating bear. Yuri heard this story and decided to join Kyokushin Karate. There are times when your life is in danger in New York, so a normal sport is not enough for self-defense. Yuri was a second-degree black belt holder in Kyokushin Karate. If opportunity allowed, she wanted to have a match against Doman Yogiashi, a third-degree black belt holder in karate, and knock him unconscious. Should a U.S. Marine assault her, she was confident that she could knock him out in less than five minutes. And if the culprit was a female martial artist who seduced strong-looking men only to knock them out in street killings disguised as "self-defense," Yuri wanted to compete with her to see who was the stronger fighter.

Chief Junichi Yamasaki had a slightly different vein of thought, however. He couldn't shake the notion of an intervention, or an involvement, of a supernatural force of some sort.

In fact, he had heard a story of a peculiar nun from his colleague in Nagoya. Several years ago, at the biggest church known as Nunoike Church in the East Ward of Nagoya, a young woman made her way into the church after losing all her memory. Yamasaki was told that it was a stormy night replete with the sounds of roaring thunderstorms when the young woman came to the church. In the beginning, the woman worked at a small bookstore that sold publications by the Society of St. Paul, baked cookies with other young nuns, and sold the cookies during Sunday service. Sooner or later, without revealing her real identity, she became a professional nun. Everyone called her "Agnes." She was a 24–25-year-old woman with large, round eyes.

One day, there was a severe earthquake in Nagoya that left a large crack in the crucifix at this church. When Agnes got down on her knees and prayed, "Jesus Christ, please resurrect if that is your wish," the cross that was skewed from the earthquake became perfectly aligned and the cracked crucifix returned to its original state.

Another story went that Agnes saved a 4-year-old child who was drowning in the river by walking on the surface of the water in front of the very eyes of the child's crying mother. Video footage of Agnes practically skating on the surface of the water at sunset went viral, although her face was not clearly shown because the video was taken from behind. There was yet another incident that surprised the church. One day, Agnes asked a 90-year-old man in a wheelchair, "Do you believe in the Lord?" and dipped him into a fountain. The old man promptly disposed of his wheelchair and began to briskly walk on his feet.

Such incidents happened on numerous occasions, and before she knew it, everyone started calling her "St. Agnes."

No field of work is exempt from jealousy. The archbishop of Tokyo started promoting the idea that her miracles could be the work of a devil. He ordered Agnes to come to Tokyo. Since then, she was nowhere to be seen, and the church in Nagoya requested the police to search for her as a missing person. It was confirmed that she boarded a shinkansen bullet train that was heading to Tokyo. Yamasaki's friend hypothesized that Agnes disposed of her gray nun habit and was now hiding somewhere in the great city of Tokyo, and he told Yamasaki, "You've got to tell me if an unrealistic or improbable case breaks out."

The dots of Nagoya and Tokyo did not instantaneously connect to form a line, but in the back of his mind, Yamasaki could not stop thinking about the miraculous nun. However, the current police force couldn't solidify, or legitimize, the case without some kind of physical evidence, witness, or confession.

A gust of wind blew on the avenue near Sakurada-mon Gate. Before he knew it, autumn had arrived.

4.

"Sir," a voice called out to Junichi Yamasaki. When he turned around, he saw Yuri Okada, unusually dressed in all pink. Yamasaki was almost six feet tall, but Yuri in her platform shoes was just the right height to look like a female foreigner.

"I know I told you to dress in a way that makes us look like a couple, but dressing in all pink with a yellow scarf around your neck is absurd. You're only 25, but your title is still 'detective.' Are you going to chase down the suspect in those platform shoes?" asked Yamasaki.

"Oh my! It is you, Mr. Yamasaki, who is going to chase down the culprit," Yuri said. "I'm only disguising as your date. If needed, Kyokushin Karate turns these bare feet of mine into a killer weapon. I can't kill a human-eating bear, but if I did a flying kick right around your heart, I might just kill you. Besides, don't you think my outfit gives off the right appearance and pheromones for men to feel like being assaulted? The guys who were killed in recent cases are all well-built. Today we're scoping it out as usual while disguised, right? I could wander around aimlessly, and if there happens to be a male partner in crime, he could fall for it as if he were caught by a live decoy."

"Do what you will. Anyway, what are we doing at Yokohama Chinatown rather than a park?"

"Look over there. Do you see it? Right there. It's a famous fortune-teller who was on TV. Let's have him look into our culprit."

The two of them walked into the shop of the most elderly fortune-teller.

"Hey, do you know if I will marry this guy?" asked Yuri to the fortune-teller while she pointed to Yamasaki.

"Please write down your name, date of birth, and occupation," the fortune-teller told her.

Yuri wrote a fake name, "Sayuri Yamashita, 26 years old." She wrote down "ballet dancer" as her occupation.

The old man, who looked like a thin frog with glasses and a beard, stared into Yuri's eyes most intensely.

"You're not a good liar, huh? Look at what we have here, a female police officer," the fortune-teller said.

"Ugh, you found out. But tell me about my marriage compatibility with this guy here."

"That man is your boss who is putting his life on the line to look for a criminal. Now is not the time."

Nothing could be done to deceive the man if he pinpointed this much at first sight.

"Will I succeed in finding the culprit? Is the culprit a female or a male, or are they working together? Did you receive any inspirations that we can use as a hint?" Yamasaki asked the old man.

"I'll give you a hint if you pay an extra ¥5,000," said the old man.

"I'm not paid much. I doubt this will be reim-bursed as a work expense," Yamasaki muttered un-der his breath as he took out ¥5,000 from his wallet.

The old man cleared his throat and began to use his bamboo divination sticks.

"Hmm. The culprit is not a normal person. They're beyond gender, beyond the matter of male or female. Oh, what's more, my clairvoyance is completely blocked off. If you try to capture the culprit, you might end up dead instead."

"But I have a gun, and I can arrest the culprit for interfering with a public officer," said Yamasaki.

"It's of no use. Your funeral is next year. And now, you fake ballerina, I can see you attending his funeral service and sending him off in a black suit."

The old man ended the conversation there because he did not want to get involved with a crime and investigation.

However, he left one word of advice. "The person you are looking for is not someone you need to defeat. Grieve with that person. Further hints can only be given by a beyond-human existence."

"What do you mean by a beyond-human existence?" Yamasaki asked.

"Go to a large bookstore and look at the spirituality section," the old man said.

The two of them, Yamasaki and Yuri, were forsaken even by the fortune-teller. No additional clue was found after walking around a park in Yokohama.

Yuri suggested they go to the Yurindo bookstore. When the two of them looked around the religion section, half the shelves were occupied by books written by a man named *Ryuho Okawa*.

"A graduate of the University of Tokyo, Faculty of Law. So he is a few years ahead of Superintendent General Yamagishi who also went to the university. Let's see if we can sound out the man through Director Nakayama of the First Criminal Investigation Division."

One week later, Superintendent General Rintaro Yamagishi met in secrecy with a man who looked slightly younger than him and had the appearance of an artist in a private room in Hotel New Otani.

"Mr. Okawa, thank you very much for training me back then at the Shichitokudo Martial Arts Hall on the Hongo Campus. I am quite embarrassed that now, someone like myself is the chairperson of the Japan Kendo Federation," Yamagishi said.

"I remember your art of kendo being straightforward and orthodox," Okawa said. "But I noticed your habit of blinking right before stepping in to attack. You probably tried to keep the opponent from reading your mind, but I quickly knew what you were thinking when I looked at your big toes and the tip of your bamboo sword."

"I tried to score a *men-uchi*, but I was too late to realize you got behind me."

"You lost too easily, and since you were the first one up, we couldn't qualify for the Kanto Semifinals even if I tried to win it back. Anyway, the Kokushikan University team was pretty strong."

Just then, the fusuma door opened and a waitress walked in with a sukiyaki hot pot.

The two of them, Yamagishi and Okawa, stayed silent for a short while. When the waitress left the room, Yamagishi opened his mouth to speak once again.

"Mr. Okawa, I'd like to narrow down the criminal profiling for that serial murder case."

"Do you have faith?" Okawa asked Yamagishi. "That's the key. You won't get to the culprit if you don't have faith."

They proceeded to chat about their university days, and the two of them separately left the hotel. It was already deep into autumn.

5.

There are only two types of people in the world.

One is people who believe they have souls residing in their bodies. The other is those who "believe" that their physical bodies are their only selves and that the so-called souls, or minds, are just the workings of the brain and nervous system.

These thoughts crossed her mind as St. Agnes sat on a bench, gazing at a cosmos flower garden in the park.

Even though she changed out of her nun habit into a denim top and a skirt, she didn't quite pass for an office worker.

Long ago, she saw a scene of *Hibiya Toshikoshi mura* (Jobless Worker's New Year Village) on TV, where people sleeping outside received food distributed during the recession. *Perhaps a kind person would lend a hand if I'm sleeping out in Hibiya Park or something*, she thought. *Or would a police officer arrest me as a runaway? I'm used to living modestly, but I don't want to meet His Excellency, the archbishop of Tokyo for him to determine whether I'm possessed by the devil.* She was feeling deeply indecisive.

So St. Agnes decided to pursue work at a flower shop named "Hibiya Kaman" for ¥900 per hour. She suffered from amnesia and couldn't remember her past, so she explained to the flower shop owner that she had studied nursing at Kinjo Gakuin Women's Junior College in Aichi Prefecture. She made up a story of her father's death and mother's remarriage as reasons to look for work in Tokyo.

She decided upon her temporary name to be "Suzu Nomura." Neither your name nor work experience mattered when working at a flower shop.

"Suzu dear, I like the way you cut the flowers," said Tae Endo, the female store manager. "When you put them in the water basin, I find beauty in your refined posture, as if you are praying. I'm sure you actually came from quite a good family. Maybe you ran away from home because your dad forced you to have an arranged marriage." Tae seemed to be a good-hearted person.

One day, there was a bag snatching incident at the park. A female office worker was on a walk during lunchtime when a man in dark clothes suddenly snatched her handbag. St. Agnes—no, Suzu Nomura—picked up a piece of wood and threw it at him. The piece didn't reach him, but the man somehow fell over. The female office worker caught up with him, and the businessmen who happened to be around her held the man down.

"God is watching, you know," Suzu muttered under her breath.

Suzu firmly believed that people who did wrong in this world deserved to be punished. She believed that was the reason why eternal souls, as well as heaven and hell, existed.

Suzu couldn't help but wonder: *even so, will God someday tell me why I was involved in a sudden accident and got amnesia from the shock?*

Back in Nagoya, why was I able to restore the crucifix that broke from an earthquake—by the power of prayer?

When I heard a mother's cry and dived into the river to save a drowning child, why was I walking on the surface of the water?

Why was the old man in a wheelchair suddenly able to walk when I asked him, "Do you believe in the Lord?" and dipped him in the fountain?

I acted righteously, and I just believed in God. Yet why do people call it the devil's power? She sighed to herself. *People are really hard to under-stand sometimes.*

As Suzu Nomura was pondering such thoughts, two men were looking over at her.

One of them, sitting on a curbstone around the fountain, was Detective Doman Yogiashi. He certainly saw Suzu throw the piece of wood at the bag snatcher. It didn't reach him, but the man fell as if a log had been caught between his legs. The offender was quickly held down by surrounding men who looked like public servants. "Perhaps…" Yogiashi began to think.

Another man was watching Suzu Nomura from a different angle. He was a tall man wearing dark shades and looked like he had come right out of *Men in Black*. He grinned.

"At last, I found you," he whispered under his breath and made a phone call.

He was Mitsuo Maejima, a member of a secret organization called MIBJ or Men in Black Japan, which belonged to the Ministry of Defense. He, too, was searching for St. Agnes, who went missing after coming to Tokyo from Nunoike Church in Nagoya. Of course, it was not to arrest her. He was on a special mission by Director General Hideki Takahashi of MIBJ to snatch her away before she was taken into police custody. Someone with rare supernatural powers could be used for military purposes or to find spies on behalf of the Ministry of Defense in Japan too. The United States, China, and Russia all use psychics to locate and raid terrorists. It seemed that MIBJ wanted to make up for Japan's lagging behind.

Meanwhile, Doman Yogiashi had received a secret order from the superintendent general to uncover the mystery of the serial murder case and find St. Agnes to gain honor for the police force.

A secret feud started between the Ministry of Defense and the Metropolitan Police Department.

6.

There was spring rain when St. Agnes arrived at Tokyo Station several months ago. Unfortunately, she did not have an umbrella. She only carried about ¥70,000 with her, so if she were to stay at a business hotel, she could only spend about 7–10 days there, including food expenses.

Agnes vaguely remembered coming to Tokyo on a school field trip a long time ago. Yet she had no memories of her parents, her school, or even her friends.

One stormy night, she was drenched by the rain and weeping as she tore her hair out and ran up a sloped street in a seemingly manic state.

Blood was running down from her thighs to her ankles. Her school uniform was ripped and thrown away somewhere, and she was only wearing a chemise. Not even wearing panties, she seemed to have been ambushed by four male students, dragged into a garage, and gang-raped. It was sad for a woman to lose her virginity to such a crime. She was filled with a confusing combination of anger and embarrassment.

Each time thunder roared in the night sky, she found herself crying out loud. "Dear God, please, kill those four damn guys." Right then, lightning struck an old cherry tree nearby. A roar of thunder echoed, and she lost consciousness.

Before she knew it, she was brought into a church where sisters were praying and caring for her. They told her that three days had passed. Her memory was gone. She was so shocked that she couldn't remember who she was. Only one thing was certain: she was saved by the church when she kept calling God's name.

"Stay here and get some rest until either your memory is restored or your family finds you," said the abbess, who was in her 60s, as she smiled gently in the morning light.

Agnes felt better after a while, and she helped the church with some cleaning or by baking cookies. Sometimes, she would pop into a church bazaar and look around to see if anyone knew her. But not a single person recognized her face. The boys who attacked her seemed to have been repeat offenders; they left no evidence behind and weren't caught by the police either.

She faintly remembered some voices.

A: "Hey, this girl's still a virgin, isn't she?"

B: "It's a pity she doesn't know guys when she's already in high school. Let's do her."

C: "I'm going first today 'cos I did well to lure her in."

D: "Hey, keep it under three minutes so all four of us can get a turn."

They ripped her clothes off, and the boys didn't let her go no matter how many times she cried, "Stop, it hurts."

There was no pleasure. To Agnes, the boys looked like devils.

A: "We won't take your life."

B: "Don't be loud."

C: "This is what all men and women do when they fall in love."

D: "This girl has a pretty face, but look, there's a bruise on her chest. It's disgusting. I definitely wouldn't make her my girl."

Crude and irresponsible words were thrown around.

No one helped me. Why does God keep these nasty guys alive? If only I had a boyfriend, at least, and he protected me... Agnes had all kinds of thoughts clinging onto each strand of her hair.

But it was all over. I'll cleanse my spirit at the church and live a new life.

Agnes cut off all interactions with the secular world and devoted her life to reading the Bible and offering her prayers to the crucifix.

The four seasons cycled several times, and her face showed no sign of hatred anymore.

As she prayed to a statue of Mary, the statue looked like it was weeping tears of blood. Perhaps it was a coincidence, but she felt that the statue was crying for her. Miracles upon miracles like those described in the Bible began to take place around her.

Some praised these miracles, but others said that it was wrong for a gang-raped woman, found fallen on the ground on a rainy day and wearing nothing but a chemise, to become a saint. The report was delivered to Tokyo, and the archbishop said he wanted to find out for himself.

How can someone like me survive in Tokyo? Agnes wondered as she stood in the rain. Just then, a flamboyant woman offered her an umbrella.

"Why don't you come over to my house today? It's a short trip to Gotanda."

Perhaps she was 27 or 28 years old. The woman had kindly invited her into her home with a hospitable voice.

Let's follow her for now, Agnes thought.

She decided to leave the rest to the heavens. The wheel of her destiny began to spin, slowly but surely. The woman from Gotanda who let Agnes stay in her apartment made instant noodles for her.

To Agnes, the white steam looked like faint hope.

7.

The woman from Gotanda was certainly kind, but she was blunt—this woman behaved almost like an elder sister. The 20-year-old apartment looked a little worn out, but the rooms were fairly clean and neat. The apartment had two rooms: a 105-sq. ft. room with a small kitchen and a 140-sq. ft. room that could either be a bedroom or a living room. It was barely enough space for two women.

Agnes asked the woman what to call her.

"Just call me Set-chan. I go by Snooping Set-suko. You're Agnes, right? I'm sure we both have special circumstances."

"What should I do?" Agnes asked.

"No need to pay," Setsuko said. "It would be nice if you could clean from time to time. I come home late sometimes, so why don't you make late-night snacks for me? I'd get sick if I only eat instant noodles. I'll leave my mega-wallet on top of the TV, so buy what you need. It only has like ¥300,000 though."

Apparently, Setsuko was a hired proprietress of a hostess bar around Gotanda, with a few others like the store manager and the bartender.

"Oh, I almost forgot. I guess I have lung cancer from smoking too much. If I pop off, do me a favor and burn my body at a public crematorium, will you? Scatter the ashes in Tokyo Bay. You're a nun, aren't you? You must have escaped from some church. Or I guess you could be wearing a uniform from an Akihabara-style nun's fashion café."

"I don't know what you mean by Akihabara-style. But it's true that I escaped from a church."

Agnes briefly explained how she seemed to have been assaulted by some guys, how she fainted after lightning struck near her, how she found herself being taken care of by the sisters at the church, and how she was called over by the archbishop of Tokyo and became a stray lamb in Tokyo. Out of extra caution, she did not mention the miracles.

"If you're a nun, I don't know if we can use you at our bar," Setsuko said. "But I admire a woman with a past. How about this? I'll lend you my clothes so you could work part-time for three hours in the evening or something. Give it a try. When I die, they might want you full-time."

"You can't die, Setsuko. I won't ever let you die. God saved my life, so I'm sure that He will save yours. You've been so kind to me."

"Oh, you should know I'm not Christian. But I worship the fox deity, Inari, for business prosperity. Sometimes I make and serve Inari sushi at the bar," Setsuko said.

After taking a day off, Agnes visited Setsuko's hostess bar called Tachibana. There were no customers yet. The only people at the bar were the store manager with a toothbrush mustache, a bartender, and two male barkers to call in potential customers.

"Set-chan, this girl's pretty good," the store manager said. "How about we market her as a princess from Ferris Girls' University who's secretly working here part-time?"

"She's pretty when she smiles. But she doesn't smile much. Maybe marketing her as a cool beauty and a dry assistant would be better," Setsuko said.

"Let's keep her professional name Natalie," the store manager said.

Just then, the doorbell rang, and a man with the appearance of a salesman and another man who looked like an ex-boxer walked into the bar.

Set-chan led the customers to a red, U-shaped couch. Hearing the manager call out, "Start with a bottle of beer," Natalie, as an overnight waitress, carried the beer to the customers through the dimly lit bar. Agnes, or Natalie, put the beer and the mugs on the table. She was about to walk away when the store manager signaled her with his eyes and made a gesture that she should sandwich the two customers with Set-chan on the other end. She didn't know what to do, but she sat down and poured beer for the customers. When she looked over at Set-chan, the latter had closed in on the salesman-looking guy. She was trying to leave no space between her thigh and his.

Five minutes passed. The doorbell rang again, and two men in black glasses walked in. They were the barkers who were inviting potential customers into the store. Each of them sat on the vacant sides of Setsuko and Natalie, preventing the two guests from leaving the U-shaped couch.

The two customers were frightened and said, "What kind of bar is this? My acquaintance told me how some place charged ¥100,000 for a bottle of beer."

In that instance, the store manager motioned for the room to be brightened up. Suddenly, the bartender had a nasty look on his face, and he urged the customers to read a poster above the entrance.

"A bottle of beer costs ¥100,000 because we have hostesses here," said the poster. Agnes, a.k.a. Natalie, would not know anything about a rigged, rip-off bar.

The salesman used to play basketball, and he was six feet tall—large for a Japanese man. The self-proclaimed former professional boxer shouted that he was a lightweight champion.

"Hey, ¥100,000 for a bottle of beer, and ¥200,000 for two bottles, is too much. This place is a rip-off."

"We put girls with you. It's not just for beer," threatened one of the barkers who suddenly put on a menacing face.

The former lightweight champion stood up, jumped over the table, and threw a right hook at one of the barkers. The man's lips split open and a drop of blood trickled down.

The manager shouted, "Here ya go," and handed over a katana to the bartender. The bartender tossed away the weapon's sheath and whipped out the lustrous blade.

"I wonder which one's stronger, your fist or my katana?" said the bartender.

The salesman thought better of the situation and promptly calmed the ex-boxer down. They left ¥200,000 on the table and hurriedly left the bar.

"Natalie, do you still think you can work here?" asked Setsuko.

"I-, I don't know what's going on…," said Agnes.

Agnes suddenly felt that she would not live with Setsuko for long.

8.

It's true that she was startled by the sequence of events at the violent, rigged bar. *It probably met the criteria for one or maybe several crimes*, she thought to herself.

Agnes, however, did not have the courage to leave Setsuko's apartment right away.

"That was nothing," Setsuko said. "We're just trying to make ends meet by efficiently taking money from dirty old men. They're all eager to touch my boobs or my ass. We're only preventing their dirty sex acts and snatching a fine."

"Won't the police come?" Agnes asked.

"The police are looking for bigger sex crimes, so only an off-duty police officer would come to Bar Tachibana to grope my boobs," Setsuko answered.

"Hmm. I also despise sex crimes committed by men, but I don't have enough knowledge to know how to punish them."

"If you don't like us running a violent bar, we can make a quick switchover to a fortune-telling bar. You have a sixth sense, don't you?"

Setsuko was spot-on. Agnes was sure that she had a spiritual ability of some sort, a supernatural power. But when it happened, it happened suddenly, and she wasn't sure if she could control her powers consciously. *Would I be able to make a correct assessment of my customers' worries and resolve them?* Agnes wondered.

Set-chan negotiated with the store manager and decided to hold off the "violent bar" for one week to experiment with a fortune-telling bar. Agnes gathered her courage and decided to go through with the fortune-telling opportunity because the guys at the bar offered to take care of any customers who might get annoyed or violent.

Setsuko prepared a mystical-looking costume for Agnes. She put on an act and set Agnes up to be "Ms. Natalie, the ex-nun fortune-teller."

Two days after that, Natalie was waiting in a special seat in the remodeled, newly opened "Tachibana Fortune-telling Bar."

The doorbell rang, and two men walked in. One was a large Black man who was a Marine, and the other was a Japanese interpreter.

The interpreter asked the store manager, "Is this a fortune-telling bar?"

"Sure is. Foreigners are welcome too. We can tell their fortunes," the store manager said.

"What about the fee?" the interpreter asked.

"Have a drink, eat some snacks, and we'll charge you ¥100,000 for a simple fortune-telling. Special fortune-telling will require tipping too," the store manager responded.

"Look at my fortunes, will you? Will I die in war, or could I have my own family someday?" asked Nichol, the Marine.

"Hey boss, this guy is an agent working to counter North Korea's missiles. Could you take a look at him?" the interpreter said.

The nearly 6′7″ Marine and Yasuzawa, the interpreter, sat in front of Natalie—the overnight fortune-teller.

Natalie put her hands together in prayer and prayed to God for a short while.

Nichol asked, "Will I die from a missile attack on our base?"

"You won't die from missiles," said Natalie.

"That's fortunate."

"But something will happen to make your parents weep, sometime this year."

"Like a traffic accident?"

"No, that's not it. You assaulted two Japanese girls while you were stationed at the U.S. military base in Okinawa. Both times you escaped back to the base without being arrested by the Japanese police."

"This guy is now at the Yokota base. How do you know he was stationed in Okinawa?" Yasuzawa asked.

"It's *ikiryo*, or the spirit of a living person. He

is possessed by the two *ikiryo* of the young girls," Natalie said.

"Yo, Nichol. What this fortune-teller is saying, is it true?" Yasuzawa asked.

Nichol didn't respond.

"There's no evidence. You're right that I was in Okinawa for some time, but I only stopped by a sex-related shop. That's all," Nichol said.

"No, you raped two high school girls. I'm sure God will punish you. Or should I say, a curse?" Natalie said.

Setsuko interrupted.

"Ms. Natalie, you'd better stop there."

"Oh, is that so? Then that will be all. After all, I don't work for the Okinawa police department," Natalie said.

Just then, the bartender put in a word to help them out. "Drink a beer, pay up ¥100,000, and make your way out the door."

"Damn it. ¥100,000 for this shitty fortune-telling. What a rip-off!" Nichol said.

"But you raped two high school girls who were opposing the U.S. military base's relocation to Henoko," Natalie said. "You even choked one girl's neck. With the other girl, you brought back her panties to the base as a trophy. The police should've been notified. Reflect on what you've done."

She hit the nail right on the head. The interpreter was terribly upset. As the first customer of Natalie the Fortune-teller repeatedly muttered, "No, I didn't do it. No," Yasuzawa, the interpreter, paid ¥200,000 including the tip.

"Thank you," Natalie said. "But watch out for the 'Cross.' The next time you assault a woman with the 'Cross,' you will surely die."

A week later, this Marine died with his arms and legs sprawled out, foaming at the mouth—at Arisugawa Park in Hiroo.

9.

After 2–3 weeks, a man with a slightly wrinkled suit and a lazily loosened tie walked in. Perhaps he was 27 or 28 years old.

"Simmered taro in sweetened soy sauce. Simmered radish with miso sauce. Fried squid rings. Give me a bottle of sake with that."

"You got it," Setsuko said as she took his order.

"You, sir, are quite old-fashioned. Or rather, an old-schooled Japanese," Setsuko added.

"Was fortune-telling ever a thing here? I remember this place used to be a hostess bar or something," the man said.

"Set-chan's body wasn't enough to bring customers in so we're changing it up," the store manager said.

"You mean this place has evolved from a rip-off bar to a scam," the man said.

"Let's not go around saying things like that," the bartender said.

"Wow, how rude," Setsuko said, as she whispered to Agnes, "Could be the police. Be careful."

"That fortune-telling thing you mentioned, is it accurate?" the man asked.

"Not only is it accurate, but it's unbelievably popular. We get more customers than ever now," the store manager said.

"Hmm. Then will the fortune-teller know anything about a missing person?"

"The amount of tip will vary depending on the importance and urgency, but you seem to be paid little so we'll make it cheap for you."

The store manager, too, had a slight sense that the man was an undercover detective.

"You can't really tell, but I'm a descendant of an onmyoji. I'm known as a descendant of Abe no Seimei. Maybe I'll have you take a look at my fortune," the man said.

"Here's Ms. Natalie, a former Catholic sister," Setsuko said.

"An acquaintance of mine died all of a sudden.

I want to know how he's doing in the other world."

"Wow, you must be quite a religious person," Natalie said.

"A number of people around me have been dying lately. I wonder if I've gotten a connection to the Grim Reaper or a *shinigami*. Is that something you can tell me?"

"Give me a moment. Let me ask God."

The man intensely stared at Natalie from top to bottom. She was pretty and gave off a slight air of a religious practitioner. But she had on an Arabian Nights-like costume, so it was hard to get an accurate sense of this.

"It's not as bad if you compare yourself to an owner of a funeral parlor, but spirits of the dead are wandering around you," Natalie said.

"What kind of spirits do you see?"

"Many of them seem to have died a sudden death."

"Maybe they were targeted by a gang. There's some bad gang called the Motoyama Family in Gotanda."

"Mr. Detective, is this for work or for pleasure?"

"Detective? Don't kid yourself. I'm thinking about quitting my job as an ordinary employee because of all the overtime I need to put in. Maybe I'll become a fortune-teller myself."

"You're not very good at lying. You're looking for the criminal, aren't you? For the unnatural deaths."

"I'm amazed that you see through so much. This is not a scam, huh. I'm a descendant of Abe no Seimei, but I have a feeling you and I are linked by fate."

"I'm an uneducated woman, so I've never heard of an onmyoji or Abe no Seimei. But I do know that you used to live in Kyoto."

"Oh, you're good. Bingo. I graduated from the Department of Religion at Kyoto University. I like religion."

"Hm, you seem to like the Internet, too."

"I like you even more. Natalie, how much do you know? Tell me."

"You heard that a 'violent bar' turned into a 'fortune-teller bar' and you came to scope me out, right?"

"Ms. Natalie, perhaps you shouldn't go out on a limb," Setsuko interrupted.

"She's right," the store manager said. "We're not a violent bar, and I swear by heaven and earth that we do nothing the police should be concerned with."

"A nun from Nagoya with mysterious powers went missing after she was called over to Tokyo. As a former sister, do you know anything about the nun in question?" the man asked.

"What are you talking about? This girl is my cousin, and she's a Tokyo-born student who attends Ferris Girls' University. She's only working here part-time," Setsuko said.

"A foreign man died in Hiroo. The Japanese interpreter who worked for him said things like 'Gotanda's fortune-telling woman' and 'the Cross,' so the police are looking into various churches. I was looking for 'Gotanda's fortune-telling woman,'" the man said.

"You're blessed by God. But it's not good to lie. I hear something like 'DOMAN ASHIA,' which I know nothing about," Natalie said.

"Yikes. My name is Doman Yogiashi, but Doman Ashiya is an ancestor of mine," the man said.

"In any case, you made a new enemy recently, so your missing person won't open their heart," Natalie said.

"Come on sir, you're going home. If you ever

plan on coming back, it will be ¥200,000, including the tip. If you're never coming back, we'll keep it at ¥50,000," the store manager said.

"You're talking to Detective Yogiashi of the First Criminal Investigation Division. This is a public service. I won't pay a single penny."

"Ah, eating and drinking without paying is a criminal offense," said the bartender. "Should we turn you in to the nearest Meguro Police Station?"

"This should be enough for today," the man said, as he left ¥2,000 on the table and hurried out of the bar.

"She seems to have an authentic supernatural ability. I don't know much more as of yet," muttered the man under his breath as he walked out in a huff.

10.

They were at a bar in Roppongi. Detectives Junichi Yamasaki and Yuri Okada pretended to be a couple while drinking bourbon diluted with water. They casually observed the bar as they concealed their presence.

"I hear that Japanese women who come here make foreigners pay for their alcohol, and later, they get hit on at the hotel," Yamasaki said.

"Which means that foreign men who come here are potential sex criminals, and the women are potential rape victims. Maybe someone here is linked to our serial killer," Okada said.

"I hate to believe that there are young girls out here who scope out foreign guys. I'd rather believe in girls with sugar daddies, girls who want middle-aged men to buy them bags and jewelry. That, I can kind of understand. Like a college girl wanting a Louis Vuitton handbag," Yamasaki said.

There was a clatter at the door, and two college girls walked in. One girl was pretty, but perhaps she ate a little too much. She was plump for a Japanese girl. The other girl was a slightly taller college student who walked in rather nervously.

Yamasaki and Okada eavesdropped on their conversation and found that the two girls had a clumsy friend whose student ID and wallet were stolen from her handbag which she carried over her shoulder while she was waiting for the traffic light on her way home at about 2 a.m. the other night.

Eventually, a Black British man and a white French man walked in. Both men were powerfully built.

The two detectives were surprised that the plump girl spoke French and the taller girl spoke English.

"Oh my, girls who can speak foreign languages come all the way to this bar to get hit on. I can't believe this," Yamasaki said disapprovingly.

"I went to school outside of Japan, and as a returnee, I feel like the English-speaking girl has a TOEIC test score of 800 at least. I mean, she can study abroad with that level of English. These girls can pick up elite Japanese men at a dating event or something," Okada said.

"I'm sorry I'm not elite."

"Don't be, Mr. Yamasaki. You graduated from the Senior High School at Komaba affiliated with University of Tsukuba, which has the highest acceptance rate into the best university in Japan, the University of Tokyo. Out of 160 students in each grade, nearly 100 of them are accepted into the University of Tokyo. As for the success rate of those getting into the University straight after graduation, your school even outnumbers Kaisei High School."

"Again, I'm sorry. I was the only one who went to the University of Tsukuba. The president back then, who even won the Nobel Prize, shouted,

'Why is there only one student enrolling from an affiliated school? I order both senior high schools at Komaba and Otsuka to move here from Tokyo,' but the high schools strongly protested against the idea and his request didn't go through. I was the only one with school spirit who went to my affiliated university."

"Oh, is that so? But Mr. Yamasaki, you are naturally bright. I heard that you also passed the exam to get into Kaisei Junior High School. You're well-known as a man who only barely missed the rank of a superintendent general."

"I reached the peak of academic performance by the end of elementary school."

"But you're an inspector in the fifth year of your career. Doesn't that mean you were hand-picked among many other candidates?"

"My friend, who is the same age as me, from Senior High School at Komaba went to the University of Tokyo's Faculty of Law and became an inspector from year one. I can't stand this. Damn it. I'll definitely win the championship at a national kendo tournament in the near future."

Just then, the plump college girl, about 21 years of age, left the bar with the French man. The taller girl was still scoping out the other guy's background in English. He seemed to be a British spy.

"Come on, you gotta pay the bill to pick up a girl if you're a spy," she said—something of that sort.

Both Yamasaki and Okada complained, "Ugh, it looks like we're going home empty-handed today."

Then, they overheard the Black British man saying how he was investigating the murder case of a U.S. Marine in Hiroo. The victim was a member of the anti-North Korean missile team, so he said the victim may have fallen for a trap from North Korea. Otherwise, he affirmed, a woman who was pushed down onto the ground at the crime scene could not have killed the Marine in a moment.

"Time for 007. Japan's Public Security Intelligence Agency must've mobilized as well," Yamasaki said.

Yuri Okada stood up and started talking to "Mr. 007" as if she was drunk. The two of them were at the bar counter.

"How do you think the Black Marine was killed?" Okada asked.

"Maybe poison injection," the British man said.

"But how?"

"North Korea uses poisonous spiders. They insert a spider's venom into a small cross at the end of a rosary and stab with it, like a needle. There was a case like that in London."

"But a Japanese athlete was killed in Odaiba, and a knife man with a criminal record was killed in Yoyogi Park. It's hard to narrow down the criminal to a North Korean spy. There is almost no relevance," Yamasaki chimed in.

"Flirting's over. You two are detectives, huh? Scary, so scary," the man said as he left the bar.

The woman left behind was stunned.

Just then, a huge explosion was heard from the Akasaka area.

The bar manager rushed to turn on the TV.

There was breaking news on NHK broadcasting.

An object that appears to be a hypersonic missile hit the prime minister's official residence. The official residence is in flames, but there are no casualties, since officials go home after 6 p.m. Prime Minister Tabata was taking a bath in the residential area when the missile struck. The bathroom glass shattered, and he suffered minor injuries from the scattered broken shards, but his life is not in danger. The Ministry of Defense, the Self-Defense Forces, and the U.S. military are currently analyzing the situation, but we know that the missile was launched from North Korea and fell on Japan after meandering for approximately 10 minutes. The Patriot Advanced Capability-3 missiles didn't make it in time. We'll report more on these details later.

Now, things were getting serious.

11.

Detective Mitsuru Noyama came to Tokyo from Nagoya in search of the missing sister. He joined Team Yamasaki.

"I met a former sister in Gotanda who acted like a fortune-teller using a sixth sense," Yogiashi said. "But she didn't look like she would commit murder. I wonder if there are gangs involved."

"Sister Agnes restored the crucifix with her psychic powers after it was tilted by an earthquake, and she even restored cracks in the statue," said Noyama. "She walked on the surface of a river like Jesus to save a drowning child. And she dipped a 90-year-old man in a wheelchair in a fountain of water while praying, and the old man started to walk briskly. People in Nagoya are talking. They're saying she might be the Second Coming of Jesus Christ or the Virgin Mary."

"Virgin Mary?" Yogiashi asked.

"That's right. The rumor goes that the statue of the Virgin Mary at the church shed tears of blood for Agnes," Noyama said.

Detective Yamasaki interrupted.

"This might be out of scope for the First Criminal Investigation Division. We would have to create a special team like *SPEC* that became both a TV show and a movie and bring in a female detective like the starring actress Erika Toda."

"I'm sorry for being an ordinary female detective," said Okada. "But I studied abroad in the States, just like Detective Touma from *SPEC*."

"There, there. Don't be so upset," said Yogiashi. "This is probably my domain as a descendant of an onmyoji. The woman from Gotanda called herself Sister Natalie, so she might not be the sister we're looking for. But her necromancy as a spiritualist seems to be real, not a scam. It's unlikely that she's a suspect, so why not invite her to the team to help us find Agnes?"

"So it's like the Tokyo edition of *Deliver Us From Evil*. Looks like I'm getting farther and farther away from the fast track," Yamasaki said.

"What are you talking about, chief? This case came directly from the superintendent general himself. If we can solve the mystery of the dead victims and catch the culprit, there's no doubt you're gonna be awarded the Superintendent General Award," said Yogiashi.

"Oh, by the way," Noyama added, "the other piece to this is that when Sister Agnes was found by the church in a chemise on a stormy night, she was so shocked from a sex-related incident that she lost her memory. I hear that she doesn't even know who she is."

"Natalie from Gotanda is a pretty girl who looks pure to me. I heard she's a Tokyo resident and is studying at Ferris Girls' University," Yogiashi said.

"Anyway, what's going on with that missile attack on the prime minister's official residence?" Noyama asked.

"We would get involved if this was domestic terrorism, but North Korea's missile attack is under the jurisdiction of the Ministry of Foreign Affairs and the Ministry of Defense," Yamasaki answered. "Apparently, North Korea is saying that it failed to launch a weather satellite, as per usual."

"It's impossible. How can they 'accidentally' hit the prime minister's official residence? This is a threat," Okada said.

"I hear they're determined to protest, but both the Ministry of Defense and Self-Defense Forces seem to be in trouble because they have lost face," Yamasaki said.

"What's the prime minister doing?" Noyama asked.

"He's curled up in fear," Yamasaki said. "Apparently, he's saying more missiles will fly at him if he stays at the hospital. That's why he's moving between different hotels every three days."

"There's also an order from the higher-ups to find North Korean spies," said Yogiashi. "The Secret Service alone is not enough. These days, even hospitals and schools are frequently under cyberattack, although these cases are still kept on the down-low."

"Yep," Okada agreed. "Withdrawals have been put on hold in eight banks. Also, medical records have been removed from a hospital in Shikoku, so they reverted back to handwritten records. What's more, last night, an elementary school nearby announced in the middle of the night, 'Fire broke out. Please calmly evacuate,' for 20 minutes on repeat. But by the time we heard fire truck sirens, they announced, 'False alarm.' I've never heard anything like this before."

"Maybe it has something to do with Russia's special military operation in Ukraine," Yamasaki said.

The four of them were talking at a barbecue restaurant in Azabu. It was also a welcome dinner for Detective Noyama who came from Nagoya.

Yamasaki received an incoming call on his cellphone that said, "Turn on the TV." He had a restaurant employee carry a small TV into their private room.

They turned on the NHK channel, and the news anchor said the following:

Three squid fishing boats off the coast of Aomori are on fire after either being attacked by jets or by mysterious objects flying in from the Northern Territories area. There's a possibility that Russia is striking back in response to the economic sanctions imposed by Prime Minister Tabata.

The prime minister is expected to secretly hold an urgent cabinet meeting at an underground shelter of the National Diet Building, but the exact location is not disclosed even to the media. Doc-

tors have revealed that the prime minister may have post-traumatic stress disorder from the recent missile attack and that as of now, he is not in a state to make an accurate judgment call.

"Oh, c'mon. Next up is Russia?" The four of them were fed up. Too many things were out of the police force's control.

12.

Cherry blossoms began to bloom around Nagoya Castle. The COVID-19 pandemic wasn't entirely over, so the cherry blossom viewers were only briefly gazing at their beauty as they walked past them. There was no sight of people reserving spots under the trees for a picnic, nor were people drinking sake under the cherry blossoms in accordance with the tradition of *hanami*.

A man, slightly past the age of 50, walked along the bank of a nearby moat. The man was Michio Taneda. A few years ago, he had quit his long-term job at *The Chucho Newspaper* to search for his daughter who had suddenly gone missing.

Taneda became a freelance writer, and his wife taught flower arrangement classes to support the household. The married couple considered getting a divorce, but it was not yet certain that the missing daughter was dead. It was even possible that she had spontaneously run away from home or perhaps eloped with her boyfriend (if she had one). She would need both parents to be waiting for her at home if and when she returned. No bodies were reported at the police station. Taneda wanted to believe that his daughter was still alive. *She must be*, he thought. She was playfully fooling around with her younger brother Norio the day before she went missing. Taneda contemplated that day when his daughter should've been in school. The weather began to go downhill in the afternoon; it started raining around the time school ended, and there was a heavy thunderstorm in the evening. Perhaps she got into an accident or an incident of some sort while waiting for the thunderstorm to subside. Taneda's daughter, Taeko Taneda, was only 18 years old. She talked about becoming a lawyer one day and adhered to a heartfelt desire to save the weak, so she had planned on applying to the School of Law at Nagoya University the following year. His daughter, a young woman with such a strong sense of justice and hope for the future, could not have suddenly been spirited away unless she got involved in an incident or accident of some kind. If she had one sin, it would've been that she was a fair-skinned beauty in Nagoya—where it is said there are not many beautiful women.

There was a slim chance of a traffic accident. Taneda traced back his daughter's usual route home from school, asking around if people knew anything and showing them a photo of his daughter. He anxiously wondered if she was abducted and sold to a sex-related business around the nightlife district in Sakae, so he went around the shops exhaustively. One man he met at a karaoke bar told him that he saw a similar-looking high school girl in a school uniform lending her shoulders to a boy with a sprained leg. Later, debris was found in an empty garage that looked like a burnt school uniform. A mattress and a blanket were also found in the garage, both revealing traces of blood that were Type A—the same blood type as that of Taeko—but DNA analysis could not confirm if the blood matched with Taeko's DNA. Other blood types were found on the mattress, and the police said the particular garage could have been used as a place to bring abducted girls and rape them. However, because there was a sudden thunderstorm the day Taeko went missing, there was not a single witness to attest to the circumstances of her disappearance. No one in the neighborhood heard anything. An old cherry tree was struck by lightning about 50 yards away from where Taeko had likely been, but no body was found.

Around then, Michio Taneda heard a rumor about the miracles of "St. Agnes." But it was hard to imagine that his daughter had suddenly become a nun. He met with the priest at Nunoike Church and showed him a photo of her, but the priest said he was not sure. The priest admitted that St. Agnes was at his church but that she suffered from amnesia and hardly seemed like a senior in high school preparing for an exam to enter the School of Law at Nagoya University. According to what he said, St. Agnes performed various miracles, but when Archbishop Ignatius of Tokyo ordered an inquiry, she fled to Tokyo, crying, "I'm not possessed by a devil." "St. Agnes is still missing," the priest said. Tokyo is a difficult place to find a missing person. Taneda's family followed Nichiren Buddhism, so it was hard to believe that she would suddenly become Christian. Besides, it was way too difficult to accept that she became not only a Catholic nun but one who performed various miracles.

However, the guys who assaulted Taeko on the stormy night must be out there somewhere. Was it possible for a person to go mad to the point of having amnesia following a traumatic experience like that?

He also met with Detective Mitsuru Noyama, whom he had known through his interview for *The Chucho Newspaper* back then. Noyama had heard of the miraculous sister, but the police were not to get involved because it was a matter within the church. The missing daughter was certainly a police-related matter, but it was not his place to get involved unless there was a possibility of murder. Noyama said that he would look into the case if they found a dead body. He promised that he would ask the First Criminal Investigation Division in Tokyo if they knew anything because he had plans to go to Tokyo.

"Taeko, Taeko, Taeko. Where are you? Are you still okay?" Every day, Michio Taneda asked around for his missing daughter, as if he were praying. Finally, he couldn't stand it. He went to Tokyo and moved around from one Internet café to another, continuing to look for Taeko or anyone who knew of her.

Meanwhile, St. Agnes left Setsuko's apartment following the incident wherein a detective stopped by the "fortune-telling bar" in Gotanda. Around that time, she started a part-time job at the flower shop Hibiya Kaman—a job opening she found during her walk along Hibiya Park. She had her hair cut short and, to alter her face, put on makeup that made her look like she had a dark tan. The part-time job at the flower shop seemed to be a better fit for Agnes than the average person because of her mother, who had taught flower arrangement classes.

Yet Agnes remembered that Detective Doman Yogiashi might have noticed her throwing a piece of wood at the purse-snatcher and the purse-snatcher subsequently tripping over. The piece was nowhere close to reaching him, so it could be seen as a coincidence that the criminal fell down, but she needed to be cautious because the detective called himself a descendant of an onmyoji.

And she also remembered feeling that she was being stared at by a tall man decked out in a black outfit with black shades for some unknown reason.

Why did I end up like this? Agnes thought to herself. *I don't know who I really am. I don't know why miracles happen to me. I don't even know why I can use psychic power. Should I meet with Archbishop Ignatius at the Tokyo headquarters and have him judge whether the miracles were the workings of the devil? Surely if I opened up about the lightning that struck on a stormy day, the gang-rape by four young boys, or the statue of Mary shedding tears of blood, he would say that I am possessed by the devil. Catholics today are no longer open-minded. This is especially true when it comes to spiritual power or supernatural ability. Bishops and archbishops who have zero spiritual powers despite their high ranks only manage affairs and administrative work within the organization. I am sure that they will send a letter to the*

Vatican and that the Vatican would ask me to take a psychiatric examination at the hospital. The worst-case scenario is for me to be excommunicated from the church.

I'm in trouble. Jesus Christ, Holy Mary, please save me. Please keep me away from all evil and guide me in the right direction.

Agnes, being sought out and needed by many, struggled with her own self-exploration.

Just then, a red carp jumped out of a pond in Hibiya Park and made a giant splash, spewing a spray of water.

13.

It was drizzling. St. Agnes, a.k.a. Suzu Nomura, was restlessly looking around as she walked down Ginza. Ginza has many businesses related to nightlife, and most of these businesses use flowers, so there are said to be over a thousand flower shops. *There must be at least one shop that would be kind enough to accept me*, she thought to herself, hoping to find new employment.

Just then, someone tapped her left shoulder from behind.

St. Agnes turned around and saw a familiar face.

"Sister Margaret."

"It's been a while. I found you by chance. I can't believe you're strolling around here."

Sister Margaret was a central figure who took care of Agnes back at the church in Nagoya. Judging by her appearance, she seemed to be five or six years older than Agnes.

"We were guided by God. I'm here for training too," Margaret said.

"Are you really here for training?" Agnes asked.

"Training is an excuse. As you can imagine, the archbishop asks about you every single day."

"I'm sorry you're having a hard time over my personal matter."

"What in the world have you been doing? For now, I can't answer all his questions. You should go say hello."

"Do you think I'm possessed by the devil?"

"The most important thing is for you to be safe. Don't worry, I'll protect you."

"I guess it'll be confessions. After that, maybe I'll be examined by a mental hospital and kept under surveillance at a nunnery for the rest of my life."

"We're living in a different age now from the young girl who discovered the Fountain of Lourdes or the young girl who heard the prophecies of Fatima. I'm sure they'll respect your rights a little more."

"Oh, Jesus Christ, please protect me," prayed Agnes.

Thus, either by chance or by the guidance of God, Agnes was to meet Archbishop of Tokyo Ignatius, accompanied by Margaret. The church was on the outskirts of Ginza. They entered the building, took the elevator up to the fifth floor, and headed for Archbishop Ignatius' room. Agnes' habit was prepared by Margaret.

The archbishop was seated in a wooden rocking chair.

The two of them took a seat on a burgundy sofa nearby.

"You must be Agnes," Ignatius said.

"Yes. That's the name I used to go by. Now I'm working part-time at a flower shop under the name of Suzu Nomura," Agnes said.

"Did you ever see Jesus Christ or any angels?"

"I'm not sure. But I felt light coming down from heaven, and I also felt like I was in an ecstasy."

"Have you ever seen the devil?"

"Not directly. Although I have had nightmares at times."

"Are your nightmares memories of you being attacked by those four boys or being struck by lightning during the storm?"

"Maybe so. Sometimes, I suddenly wake up in the middle of the night, fearful, with tears in my eyes."

"What do you do then?"

"I ask the Lord God to save me, or I often call the name of Jesus Christ."

"Do you consider yourself a child of God?"

"No, I think I'm a sinful person. My memories from the past haven't returned yet, and I wish to ask the Immaculate Mary for forgiveness for my involvement in a sex crime, for creating four sinners."

"Is it true that the statue of the Virgin Mary at the church in Nagoya shed tears of blood?"

"It's only a rumor. I'm not certain."

"Is it true that the crucifix, tilted by an earthquake and partially destroyed, was restored by your prayer?"

"That, too, I can't confirm myself. I'm not sure."

"Is it true that you walked on the surface of a river to save a drowning child?"

"It's true that I was desperate to save him, but the video footage that spread on the Internet may be fake. It could've been edited by someone."

"Is it true that you healed a crippled elderly man by praying and baptizing him with water?"

"I'm sure that is not my power but the power of those who believe in the church."

Agnes was becoming a little tired, and she felt light-headed. A woman who was making money at a "fortune-telling bar" until recently shouldn't be having an intense, and practically interrogative, back-and-forth dialogue with the archbishop.

Margaret put her arms around Agnes' waist in support.

"Your Excellency, I'm a sinful laywoman. Please allow me to live a life of an ordinary girl." Agnes, having said this, suddenly lost consciousness.

The archbishop said, "We'll end it there for today," and he let her go.

Margaret left the church and took Agnes to a cheap business hotel.

The archbishop was stricken with a sense of helplessness and bewilderment.

How could such a girl perform miracles like that of Jesus and Mary when I, the archbishop in charge of this great city of Tokyo, am not given any spiritual ability? The archbishop thought to himself. *If the miracles are true, I could consult the Vatican so that Agnes could be recognized as a saint. Yet I can't understand why she was given a spiritual ability after being assaulted by the boys and losing her virginity. Under normal circumstances, it wouldn't be surprising for her to invite the devil out of vengeance. The way in which she was carried into a church after being knocked out by lightning is also unacceptable because it sounds too Protestant; it's too similar to the story of Martin Luther, the Protestant reformer, when he entered the monastery. I'd better relinquish any empathy for the girl and investigate her further, with greater discernment.*

However, early the next morning, Suzu Nomura, a.k.a. St. Agnes, fled the hotel. She was scared out of her mind.

14.

St. Agnes, a.k.a. Suzu Nomura, escaped from Ginza and got off at Futako Tamagawa Station. She bought cheap clothes sold at half the original price at a nearby Takashimaya department store— a navy retro dress with a white polka dot pattern of 70s or 80s style. Along with the dress, she put on an affordable navy hat made of cloth and a pair of non-prescription, tortoiseshell glasses. *With this look, surely no one will recognize me at first sight*, she thought.

After eating a light meal of curry, Suzu strolled alongside the Tama River. *Today, I won't be hard on myself no matter what happens. I'll just spend the day relaxing and freeing myself from stress*, she thought.

Suzu saw several 40-inch-long black carp from the top of the bridge. She felt a sudden urge to walk alongside the river, and she strolled along the riverbank. Several people riding bicycles passed her by. A young lady was jogging toward her from the opposite direction. Suzu felt that this was a safe location.

Just then, a screeching cry echoed. Suzu went straight toward the cry.

The cry came from a dense field of tall grass. A high school girl wearing a white top with a burgundy scarf and a navy-colored skirt was surrounded by four boys that looked like prep school students. Suzu felt a sudden rush of blood to her head. *It's happening again. They're beasts, not men. Do they think it's okay to take away a girl's future just to fulfill their animalistic sexual needs? Do they think God will forgive them again and again?* Suzu, no, St. Agnes, was surprised to find herself feeling like St. Agnes once more.

She was also surprised to find herself going down the riverbank without a second thought, free of any inhibitions.

Just then, the young lady from earlier who was on a run, wearing a black jogging suit with white stripes down her pants, also rushed down the riverbank.

"Y'all should feel ashamed!" the jogger lady shouted as she approached the four men. A man hovering above the girl turned his neck. The lady's spinning kick made a clean strike to the temple of his head, incapacitating the man with slanted fox-like eyes who was about to rape the helpless girl. It was a clean low kick.

The man literally flew away after being kicked in the head. She then landed a flying kick into the chest of a 6-feet-tall man with a face like a potato. The potato-like man blew a bubble of saliva and was instantly knocked unconscious. The third man, who seemed like he would make a great sumo wrestler, ungracefully grasped at the jogger lady from behind. For a brief moment, the lady acted as though she intended to run away but then threw a clean back kick with her heel sinking into the man's crotch. The man fell over to the right in anguish as he tried to protect his balls with both hands and avoid another agonizing blow to his crotch. The lady was clearly experienced in karate or kung fu.

While the three men were being beaten up, a tall man in shades, clearly the leader of the pack, grabbed a metal baseball bat from his motorcycle, which he had laid down beside the riverbank. Metal bat in hand, he ran over and aimed for the lady's head.

The lady quickly rolled down to the grass on her side and dodged the swinging blow of his bat.

Oh my! Agnes stretched out both arms, opened her palms, and said a prayer. "O Lord, may You give us power."

Astonishingly, the metal bat, which cut through the air and hit the ground, cracked into three pieces.

The jogger lady, who had rolled horizontally, watched Agnes the entire time. "So she has psychic powers," she murmured.

The man with the metal bat furiously ran toward Agnes and forcefully pushed her down. After throwing her some left and right punches, the man ripped apart her newly bought navy dress with both hands. He tore off her bra.

Just then, his eyes caught sight of something black. Between her breasts was a cross-shaped bruise. As soon as he laid eyes on the cross-shaped bruise, the tall man's eyes rolled back and he was instantly knocked out, with foam frothing at his mouth.

The jogger lady ran over. She took his pulse. "Nothing." It was an instantaneous death.

The lady's name was Yuri Okada, a detective and a second-degree black belt holder in Kyokushin Karate.

Yuri took a deep breath. "For now, I'll call the cops and ambulances," she said, and she proceeded to make calls on her cellphone.

"Thanks for helping me," she told Agnes after calling in the incident. "The guy looks dead, but regardless of the cause of his death, I'll explain that it was self-defense. No need to worry."

Yuri helped the high school girl, still lying on the ground, to get up. The girl was still in shock from the violence and attempted rape.

Yuri looked back at Agnes and said, "Police cars from Tamagawa Station will come soon, along with ambulances. Were you hurt?" Everything happened in the blink of an eye. Agnes' head was spinning.

"I'm a detective. I'll handle things smoothly. Tell the Tamagawa police officers about the attempted assault on the two of you and nothing else. I'm glad you weren't injured," Yuri said.

"Um, am I guilty of murder?" Agnes asked.

"Let's just say that the guy had a heart attack while you were wrestling with him in self-defense. That should be good enough, Agnes," Yuri said.

Agnes was surprised by the female detective's skillful use of Kyokushin Karate, but she was even more taken aback by this lady's high level of intuition to figure out who she was.

Later on, Yuri's colleagues also came by while Agnes was formally investigated by the police at Tamagawa Police Station.

The colleagues were Team Leader Junichi Yamasaki and Detective Doman Yogiashi along with Detective Mitsuru Noyama, who was visiting Tokyo from Nagoya.

The police officers condemned the three men who tried using violence, saying, "Don't underestimate a female detective. How could you possibly beat her?"

"And yet," said Nakamura, a senior police officer at Tamagawa Police Station, as he turned to Yuri, "You beat one man to death?" Yuri responded, "He probably had a chronic disease or something. Maybe it was a heart attack."

"Why is the metal bat broken into three parts? Is Kyokushin Karate that powerful?" Kimizuka, another police officer, asked.

"Yes. I mean, they can cut the neck off of a beer bottle barehand," Chief Yamasaki played along.

Doman was surprised to see Agnes. He shut his mouth after Yuri motioned him to shush.

"Say hello to the director for me. We'll take care of this young lady who assisted Detective Okada," said Yamasaki as his team quickly left.

St. Agnes was now turned over to Team Yamasaki of the First Criminal Investigation Division.

Maybe it's the murder, Agnes vaguely wondered while riding in the police car.

15.

St. Agnes, a.k.a. Suzu Nomura, arrived at the Tokyo Metropolitan Police Department Headquarters near Sakurada-mon Gate for the first time. Team Yamasaki wanted to conduct a highly confidential interrogation before the official joint investigation meeting of the serial murder case.

Junichi Yamasaki, as the head of Team Yamasaki, chief, and inspector, faced Suzu Nomura.

Yuri Okada sat at her desk behind Yamasaki, forming a right angle, and typed up the conversation transcript on a computer.

"This will be kept as a secret investigation until the full details of the unique cases are revealed," Yamasaki said. "You were asked to come here voluntarily, so this doesn't mean you were arrested. But this case links with several other cases that the police are investigating, so I apologize for a few days of inconvenience, as you're a material witness."

"Am I a murderer?" Suzu asked.

"Instead, I would like to first thank you," Yamasaki said. "Thanks to your ability, Detective Okada wasn't beaten with a metal bat. Even a third-degree black belt holder of Kyokushin Karate could've had a few broken bones from being bludgeoned with a metal bat."

"Um, I'm a second-degree black belt holder," Okada chimed in. "A third-degree holder is said to be able to kill Antonio Inomoto (pro-wrestler) in his prime."

"Well, well, small details aside, Detective Okada testified that when you extended your arms out and opened your palms while reciting some spell, the metal bat of Tanimoto, the leader of the pack, broke into three. This is an eyewitness account from a detective, so it's reliable, and certainly, the metal bat taken as evidence was actually broken into three pieces. According to the crime lab, a metal bat can't be broken with just three hits, even by the hammer of a professional woodcutter. Detective Okada says you're a psychic."

"What's a psychic?"

"It's a so-called superhuman, someone with a spiritual ability or supernatural power."

"I don't know what you mean. I only prayed to the Lord. As for the power that comes with a prayer, you'd better ask the descendant of an onmyoji, who is listening on the other side of that one-way mirror."

"So you're clairvoyant too. Can you see Detective Yogiashi on the other side of the mirror?"

"There's also a detective from Nagoya, along with a higher-up, Director Sugisaki, and the head of the First Criminal Investigation Division, huh."

There was a stir on the other side of the mirror glass. "She might be real," said the director.

"That's why it's a matter of onmyoji," said Detective Yogiashi.

"Actually, we are racking our brains over three incidents," Yamasaki regained his calm. "The first is the murder of a U.S. Marine at Arisugawa Park in Hiroo. The second is the murder of an athlete in Odaiba. The third is a murder case in Yoyogi Park. Actually, it's not even confirmed whether these cases were murders. They're all fatal cases though. All three men were well-built, and it's as if they were suddenly taken away by a shinigami just as they were about to rape women. Do you know anything about this?"

"Oh, Mr. Yamasaki, you are such a gentleman. Why don't you ask me directly if I did it?"

"The cops won't label a good citizen as a murderer without any evidence. But it was so sudden how Tanimoto, the leader of the four brats, died on the riverbank by the Tama River. I sensed a similarity."

"I have no weapons, and I can't do karate. He died, just like that. I have been a devoted sister for several years; I can't just suddenly switch into a bloodthirsty killer, if that's what you're implying."

"We know you're called St. Agnes. We've also heard rumors about the various miracles you performed. But these are just internal matters of the church. Unless we can file a fraud case, we, the police, can't interfere, since the freedom of religion is guaranteed by the Constitution of Japan. It's not up to the police to decide whether miracles can happen in the present age or not."

"I don't remember anything until the age of 18. I go by Suzu Nomura now, but I don't know my birth name either. It seems that I was assaulted by four young men on a night of a terrible thunderstorm. They haven't been caught yet. I'll help with your investigation if the four criminals are caught."

"That means you'll help us by offering your psychic ability for the criminal investigation, right? That's how I'll become a 'Tokyo Psychic Investigator,' much like *Deliver Us From Evil*."

"What's that?"

"There's a movie called *Deliver Us From Evil*. Apparently, supernatural powers and psychic abilities are used to help investigate murder cases in New York. Japan hasn't officially implemented something like that yet and everything is still based on forensic evidence."

"Well, I'm so tired today. Could we call it a day and continue tomorrow?"

"OK. Detective Okada, do you have a special shelter for her?" Yamasaki called over to Okada.

"There's a women's dormitory for the Bank of Japan near Shibuya, and there's a shelter for women behind it," Okada said. "It's within the premises of the Bank's dormitory, so no one will find out there are people related to the police living there. The Bank of Japan is heavily guarded. No gangs or thieves can break in. We just need to have a female police officer dressed in plain clothes."

"Alright, we'll have her live there for a few

days. Could you take care of her change of clothes and food?" Yamasaki asked.

"Will do," Okada said.

Agnes was released around 11 p.m. She earnestly wanted a good night's rest at the shelter. She was too drained after reaching both her physical and mental limits with the events of the day.

16.

That night, Agnes couldn't sleep well. There was that incident by the Tama River, and she was taken into a police car. It wasn't an official arrest, but it didn't change the fact that she was taken into custody. She was virtually being treated as a suspect.

Agnes was so tired that she eventually fell asleep a little after 1 a.m. Yet she wasn't able to sleep well, and she was faintly awake around 3:30 a.m.

It happened just then. Someone straddled her over her thin blanket, and black hands began to strangle her. She couldn't move her body. She felt a heavy weight pushing down on her chest and stomach. Of the hands choking her, the right hand grasped the upper part of her throat, while the left hand grasped the lower part.

This was the so-called sleep paralysis. That's how Agnes understood it.

Agnes opened her eyes wide and clear. She was not dreaming. The thick curtains of her room were open, leaving just the lace curtains closed. Moonlight was faintly shining into her room. *The thing that is holding me down, is it a burglar?* The fact that two black arms were choking her neck, the fact that it had a shadow-like head, the fact that it had a body but was translucent from the waist down—

It can't be human, she thought.

At that moment, she heard a man's voice.

"You made a wish on the stormy night. You said, 'Dear God, please, kill those four damn guys,' didn't you?"

The shadow man had two horns growing from his head. His eyes were an eerie blackish-red. Fangs protruded from his mouth: two from the top and two from the bottom.

"I'm afraid that even though I'm a god, I'm a god who brings death or a shinigami. In Nagoya, you prayed to God while screaming, so I killed off four men in Tokyo for you. All four were the same kind of beast-like humans whose sole purpose was rape. They don't deserve to live. It's only natural for them to be taken to the other world. I'll send them down to the Hell of Beasts and have them born as animals in their next lives. They'll be shot dead by hunters or slaughtered and eaten like pigs and cows. There, are you happy? This is the answer to your prayer to God."

Agnes gasped and spoke with the voice of her heart.

"If I killed someone, I'm the one to atone for my sins. I never intended to hire a shinigami."

"Yes, yes, you were a role model until your senior year of high school. You wanted to become a lawyer and save the weak, huh. Look what happened. Neither the God of Christianity nor Jesus helped you. Your school uniform was ripped apart by four men, and they took, by way of gang rape, the virginity that you carefully protected. Not even one in 10,000 people lose their virginity like this. I'm sure the murder in Hiroo, the murder in Odaiba, the murder in Yoyogi Park, and now the murder by Tama River are not enough to get rid of your resentment. Do you also want me to kill the four rapists who assaulted you? You even paid the price of amnesia. You lost your family. You lost hope. All you have is vengeance," the shinigami said.

"It looks like you're not an ordinary shinigami," Agnes said. "You're a devil. I had a sad past, but lightning struck an old cherry tree and I lost consciousness. After that, I was brought back to life by the good care of kind people, and thanks to the power of God, I became a nun with the name of 'Agnes.' God never abandoned me. Besides, I came to be endowed with a mystical power that's hard to explain myself. I'm truly happy that I found religion."

"Oh, that's a nice mindset," the devil said. "But your dear archbishop of Tokyo has become jealous. He wants to conclude that your spiritual powers come from the devil, so you can't go back to the church anymore. You've escaped, after all. Are you planning to live your life as a deceiving fortune-teller? Or as a part-timer at a flower shop? Or are you going to be sentenced to death as a serial killer responsible for four deaths? Whatever you decide is a petty life."

"Please stop. My thoughts and actions dictate my life. Even if you're truly a shinigami or a devil, it's not the spiritual beings in the other world that would dictate my life."

"You seem to have grown a bit for a lass. But you know, your father quit working for a large newspaper company after you disappeared. He's looking for you around Nagoya and Tokyo under the guise of being a freelance journalist. Your father's name is Michio Taneda, former deputy chief editor of a major newspaper. He's on the verge of getting a divorce because your parents got on bad terms with each other as they kept looking for you. Your younger brother, Norio, was it? He quit high school before graduation and is doing part-time newspaper delivery and working at construction sites. Your mother, Nobue, used to teach flower arrangement, but after she tried to hang herself once, she lost her students because they were creeped out. There's another thing. The other day, your father bought a kitchen knife. He's planning on stabbing the rapists to death if he finds them while he looks for you."

"That's enough. I don't want to hear the words of a devil. I don't want to hear a voice other than that of Jesus Christ, of the Virgin Mary, or of the Lord God whom Jesus loves. Away with you, Satan!"

The night slowly dawned into day.

There was a knock at the door, and a female police officer in plain clothes offered Agnes breakfast.

"We'll prepare an inconspicuous car for around eight o'clock, so please head over to Sakurada-mon Gate. Detective Okada will come to pick you up," said the female police officer.

"Please send word that I have something to talk about today with Detective Doman Yogiashi," Agnes told her.

At 7:55 a.m., a van quietly stopped near the dormitory of the Bank of Japan in Daikanyama.

Day two began.

17.

Doman Yogiashi was already waiting in the interrogation room. Behind him, Yuri Okada started preparing her station at a steel desk to record the conversation onto a computer.

"Thank you very much for requesting me," Yogiashi said.

Yamasaki and the others were watching them from behind the one-way mirror. Agnes started speaking:

"Could you help me organize my thoughts? I couldn't sleep well because from around 3:30 a.m. I was attacked by first a shinigami and then a devil. I thought you'd give me some tips to figure things out. You graduated from Kyoto University's Department of Religion and are a descendant of an onmyoji, right? I think you know a lot about spiritual matters."

"Yes, I think I understand the basic theories of most religions—Buddhism, Japanese Shinto, Christianity, Judaism, and Islam," Yogiashi said.

"Do spiritual punishments and curses really exist?"

"They certainly do exist. My family still works as a modern onmyoji in this Reiwa period. My father is a Shinto priest on the surface, but in reality, as the 36th generation of Doman Ashiya, he repels spiritual punishments and curses and conducts ritual prayers for marriage or the recovery of illness. I'm told to take after my father as the 37th generation when I quit this job as a detective. He always tells me that there must be a bunch of spirits of the dead and ikiryo, or spirits of the living people, in the division that I work for, since it gets a lot of murder cases."

"Detective Doman," Okada chimed in. "Do you really want to keep this on record? I don't want weekly gossip magazines to write about us as 'Spiritual Detectives.' Mr. Yamasaki will scold you later."

"There, there. It's my family's occupation and I want a real talk with Ms. Agnes here. It should be fine," Yogiashi said.

Agnes wiggled her legs around restlessly as she stared down at her black pantsuit and white sneakers. After a brief period of silence, she opened her mouth to speak.

"That shinigami said he took the lives of four people at Hiroo, Odaiba, Yoyogi, and now Tama River. He said he killed them because when I was assaulted in Nagoya, I cried, 'Dear God, please, kill those four damn guys.' So, the shinigami killed the four. Can you believe that? Can murder even be projected onto someone else in that way?"

"Hm, this matter is beyond the police. Arresting a shinigami for murder only happens in comic books. I'm rather interested in whether people die instantly if you wish for that to happen, Agnes. From an onmyoji's point of view, it could happen to a 'superman' at the level of Abe no Seimei, but modern science can't possibly prove its cause and effect. Each corpse was lying on its back with its eyes rolled back and foaming at the mouth, so you could say it was similar to the demonic possession in the movie, *The Exorcist*. But it is a movie after all. It's hard to determine which scenes are real and which ones are purely fictional. If the deaths were caused by your curse, the four who raped you should've died from something like a traffic accident, suicide, or arson."

Okada cleared her throat. "Mr. Doman. This is the Metropolitan Police Department, not a shrine."

"In any case, we can't explain the connection between the four men in Nagoya and the four men in Tokyo. So you admit that you were gang-raped before you became a nun in Nagoya?" Yogiashi asked Agnes.

"My memory isn't entirely reliable, but I believe that's when I became a sister at the church under God's guidance."

"Is there anything else you're bothered by?"

"The shinigami, or the devil who caused my sleep paralysis, mentioned how I wanted to be a lawyer, how my father quit his job as a news reporter to search for me and the rapists in Nagoya and Tokyo, how my mother attempted suicide, and how my younger brother dropped out of high school and is now delivering newspapers. But in Catholicism, we're told not to listen to the devil's words during an exorcism, so I just prayed and prayed for him to be gone. I'd fall into the enemy's trap if I allowed my mind to be disturbed."

"The police will take care of that and see if there is anyone who matches your description," Yogiashi said. "The only concrete evidence we currently have is how you tried to save Detective Okada by the Tama River; how you extended your arms out and prayed; how the metal bat of the fourth, boss-like man broke into three pieces and the detective was saved; and how he went so mad that he tried to rape and murder you but instead died instantaneously without any visible injuries or weapons involved. And finally, we know that this detective here saw the whole sequence of events from beginning to end."

"I wonder if God or Jesus Christ saved me."

"The Identification Division experts are interested in the metal bat as physical evidence, the bat that was broken into three pieces. There's an anecdote that you should know. When a Buddhist monk named Nichiren was about to be beheaded as a criminal at Yuigahama beach in Kamakura, the executioner's sword suddenly crumbled into pieces. They could not chop off his head. This had actually been predicted in the Kannon Sutra in the Lotus Sutra of Buddhism. It describes the spiritual merit of believing the Lotus Sutra—that when someone tries to cut off the head of its practitioner, the sword falls apart."

"Does that mean I received the power of the Goddess of Mercy or the power of angels?"

"That's what I'd like to believe. Unfortunately, today's police, judges, and prosecutors don't believe in anything that falls outside of laws or legal documents. On my end, it would be much easier to understand the case if the metal bat was broken by Detective Okada's high kick and if the man died an instant death with her punch to the pit of his stomach."

Detective Yuri Okada got furious. She slammed her computer shut and stood up.

"How dare you say such a thing, you damn pseudo-monk. You say I'm a murderer? You think I kill bears? You think I'm an alien?? I'm going to kill you, right here, right now. Let's make it clear who's stronger, a second-degree black belt holder of Kyokushin Karate or a third-degree black belt holder of the Japan Karate Federation!"

Detective Yamasaki opened the door in a flurry and stepped in. The director was worried that this case would remain unsolved.

18.

A doctor was called over from the Police Hospital to a private room in Hotel Okura to avoid drawing unwanted attention. There, Agnes was taking some rest until a slightly bald man named Doctor Kikuchi walked in along with Detectives Yamasaki and Okada. Later, they were joined by Detective Yogiashi, who was wearing a sweater. The room was furnished in a slightly old-fashioned, chilled-out style, with a burgundy carpet, wooden chairs, and a deep brown sofa. A couch bed had also been prepared for Agnes.

Generally, a scientific diagnosis by a doctor should be required. But since it was not possible with the ongoing case, a psychiatrist was arranged to conduct a hypnotic regression to retrieve Agnes' forgotten past and collect both audio and video recordings. The team wanted concrete evidence that they could hand over to the court—evidence that was more reliable than the judgment made by an onmyoji.

"Alright, Ms. Suzu Nomura. I'll be conducting a hypnotic regression so we can revive your memory, even if just a little," Dr. Kikuchi said. "I'll slowly hypnotize you and gradually trace your memory back to your younger days. Please relax and follow my guidance. Mr. Yogiashi and Ms. Okada will help me record this session, but your privacy will be protected from the public. This is only to investigate the cause of your amnesia and understand what actually happened to you. I've done this more than 500 times on other patients without even a single accident, so you can trust me. In the unlikely event of an emergency, or if you feel sick, I'll immediately stop the hypnotic regression and bring you back to normal."

"Alright. What should I do?" Suzu asked.

"Lean back on the couch bed to about 30 degrees and relax, will you?"

Suzu did just as she was told. Detective Doman was in charge of the audio recording, and Detective Yuri was in charge of the video recording; both of them were starting to feel nervous, but they tried to relax after the doctor signaled to them with his eyes.

Dr. Kikuchi, dressed in a white lab coat, took out what looked like a pocket watch from one of his pockets and held out his right arm, pinching the end of the chain with his fingers to hold it like a pendulum. He guided Suzu to keep her eyes on the round watch.

"I'm going to count down from ten. As I count, you'll fall into a deep sleep. Ten, nine, eight, seven, six, five, four, three, two, one. Now, your eyelids are getting heavy, and you are falling into a deep sleep," Dr. Kikuchi said.

Suzu gradually began to doze off into a deep sleep.

"You're in your last year of high school. You're walking back home. On the day of the storm and lightning, what happened to you?" Dr. Kikuchi asked.

"I'm a senior at Rakuyo High School. I didn't have to go to cram school that day, so I was going to be home at a little after 4 p.m. and planned to help out my mother, Nobue Taneda, with cooking dinner. I was walking along the edge of a narrow river, and I met a male student who had twisted his ankle. He said to me, 'My house is close by. Could you lend me your shoulder?' I let him put his right arm on my right shoulder, and I put my left arm around his waist. We walked about 50 yards. Ahead of us, I saw a house with an open garage, and he said, 'Can you take me there so I can enter the house from the garage?' So I carried him inside the garage."

"Was anyone in the garage?"

"There were two people who looked like students. Another person got around behind my back and shut down the garage door. There was a naked light bulb inside the room. It started raining around that time."

"Did they say anything?"

"A student with a mohawk who seemed like the leader said, 'Stay here for a while until it stops raining.'"

"What did the boys do?"

"The boy who closed the garage shoved me from behind, and I fell down on a blue mattress."

"What did they do next?"

"The student who was limping returned to normal and said, 'You shouldn't trust people so easily. I'll punish you in the place of your daddy.' He started to take off my school uniform. I tried to fight back, but all four boys got together to rip off my school uniform, and I was left in only a chemise."

"Did they just take off your clothes?"

"I heard a voice saying, 'Guys, she's still a virgin. Let's celebrate her for her coming of age.' Another voice said, 'Only three minutes each,' and they raped me from front and back," Suzu said, as tears streamed down her face.

"So they assaulted you."

"Yes. It happened in the span of about 20–30 minutes."

"What happened next?"

"It hurt, and I saw myself bleeding. One man lifted the garage door a bit, so I ran away crying, wearing nothing but a chemise in the pouring rain. I ran about 50 yards up a sloped street and saw an old cherry tree. All of a sudden, lightning struck the tree and I lost consciousness. Before I knew it, three days had passed, and I was being taken care of at a church."

"That's how Sister Agnes was born, huh."

"That's right."

Now that Suzu's account explained the case in Nagoya, everything will align with Detective Mitsuru Noyama's investigation, thought Yamasaki.

"After you became a sister, did you use any peculiar powers?" Dr. Kikuchi asked.

"Jesus Christ and the Virgin Mary appeared in front of me several times. Jesus told me that I've been carrying a cross since I was born."

"What does that mean?"

"Ever since I was born, I had a bruise on my chest in the shape of Shikoku Island on a map, but once Jesus told me that, the bruise morphed into the shape of a cross."

"And that is when St. Agnes was born?"

"That's right. Since then, many mysterious events took place around me. But it wasn't because of my own power. It was the power of faith, of believing in Jesus."

Dr. Kikuchi ended the hypnotic regression.

The dot of Nagoya and the dot of Tokyo connected to form a line. Yamasaki thought that now he just had to collaborate with Detective Noyama to investigate her family, school, and friends and conduct an on-site inspection, like an orthodox police investigation.

From then on, she would be called by the code name, "Woman with the Stigma"—another name for "the miracle woman."

It became clear that supernatural phenomena were involved. The case would eventually develop beyond the scope of the police.

19.

Detective Mitsuru Noyama returned to Nagoya later that evening, the same day that Dr. Kikuchi conducted the hypnotic regression. Now, they knew a couple of things about Agnes: she was in her senior year at Rakuyo High School at the time of her disappearance, her mother's name was Nobue Taneda, and she became a sister at a church. *It shouldn't be hard to confirm her identity*, Noyama thought.

The first thing Mitsuru Noyama did was find Agnes' high school homeroom teacher at the time she went missing. She was a 48-year-old English teacher named Kumiko Horigai.

"Yes, it's already been six, seven years," Horigai said. "I remember Ms. Taeko Taneda very well. Her English pronunciation was beautiful. She was a lovely girl. I remember her radiant white teeth when she smiled. She had good grades, and she talked about wanting to go to the School of Law at Nagoya University and becoming a lawyer one day to help people in need. If that incident never happened, she would have graduated from law school and become a lawyer by now."

"How did she get along with others? Was she ever disliked by someone or bullied?"

Detective Noyama, with a large body that suggested he practiced judo, asked Taeko's former teacher these questions as he awkwardly took notes in his notebook.

"That's hard to imagine," Horigai said. "She was a pure and intellectual girl, a beautiful one too. She was kind and caring to everyone around her without discriminating. Still, she was not the type to seduce men or to blow hot and cold—I mean, she wasn't the type who would change her attitude to make men chase her. She wasn't the nerdy type who was isolated from the other students either. Her father was a reporter for *The Chucho Newspaper*, so she had a strong sense of justice too."

"If you were to point out one weakness of hers that could be taken advantage of by men, what would it be?" Noyama asked.

"I guess it would be sympathy," Horigai answered. "If she saw a poor wretch, she couldn't leave them be. It's not that she would get herself involved in criminal behavior but more like she would save a crying child in a house on fire even if she burnt herself or died in place of the child."

"Do you think it's possible for her to commit some kind of crime, such as murder or inflicting injury on someone, out of vengeance?" Noyama asked.

"My gut tells me there's absolutely no chance of that. She was also the president of a flower arrangement club, and when she was arranging flowers, I overheard her saying, 'Oh flower, I'm sorry if this hurts. I just want everyone to see your beauty.'"

"Let's say, and I'm talking hypothetically, that unknown men raped her—my apologies for the vulgar language, I'm a cop after all—if men assaulted her, do you think she could run away from home or become a sister to enter a nunnery?"

"She's not an irresponsible person, so she would surely consult with her parents or her friends. I can only think that her sudden disappearance was not a matter of the school or her family, but it had to do with some incident or an accident," Horigai said.

Noyama asked her to list out the names of Agnes' old friends, both male and female, and later spoke with each of them. Their testimonies more or less aligned with the description given by her homeroom teacher. She wasn't the kind of girl who would make enemies or elope with a man. She was about 5′2″, Noyama learned, along with the fact that she played soft tennis in junior high school.

Noyama also met her mother, Nobue Taneda. Bluntly put, she looked more weathered than her actual age would have indicated. He felt her stress and worries that had accumulated over the past few years. She worked her flower arrangement job twice a week, but she currently only had three or four students. Her husband, Michio Taneda, had quit his job to become a freelance journalist, but since his income was unstable, they were in financial trouble. Agnes' younger brother, Norio, dropped out of high school in his first year, and he was now hopping around from one part-time job to another.

"Mr. Detective, did you find out anything?" Nobue asked hopefully.

"Ms. Taeko Taneda is with us. She's doing well. Unfortunately, she is now suffering from amnesia and can't remember anything before the age of 18."

"Can she meet her family members right away?"

"The police are investigating her relationship with a series of serious crimes. She can't meet with you right away."

"Oh no, my child, of all people, to get involved in serious crimes…"

Nobue's face turned pale, so Noyama didn't mention the murder cases. He moved on to his next task of on-site inspection.

The house where Taeko Taneda was thought to have been gang-raped had deteriorated but still existed. The Identification Division team concluded from the garage investigation that although there was no murder or inflicted injury, a virgin might have been raped there, based on the amount of blood remaining on the blue mattress. Even so, it was hard to identify the assailants. Noyama also confirmed the location of an old cherry tree that looked like it was struck by lightning about 50 yards from there, up a sloped street. *Taeko must have run away here in the rain, encountered a lightning strike, fainted, and lost her memory*, he thought.

Noyama continued to conduct interviews at the nunnery of a large church and found that a woman around the same age as Taeko was once protected and cared for by the church and that she helped out around the nunnery. He showed them a recent photo of Taeko. Several people recognized her, but they claimed that on that stormy night, Taeko was not wearing a school uniform and no one knew who she was. When Noyama asked about the miracles of St. Agnes, they all kept mum. The miracles seemed to be a secret of the church that couldn't be openly shared with a layman.

Meanwhile, at the shelter in Daikanyama, Tokyo, Taeko Taneda was reflecting on all kinds of events: an unexpected gang rape, family and friends that she couldn't recall, the lightning strike on a stormy day, how she became a sister at a church, and how she was now suspected to be a serial killer.

Even the archbishop of Tokyo did not acknowledge for a raped woman to be worshiped like the Virgin Mary. *Maybe I received the power of the devil*, Taeko wondered, and she asked Detective Doman Yogiashi a question. She was counting on his expertise in religion.

"Do you think a woman who became a victim of a crime is bound to become a femme fatale, targeted by the devil, instead of meeting God or angels?"

Hearing this, Doman Yogiashi recounted the story of the Buddhist Uppalavanna. Uppalavanna was a renowned female disciple of Shakyamuni Buddha, but because of her beauty, she was raped by several male disciples who were hiding underground when she returned from collecting alms one evening. Of course, the male disciples were expelled from the priesthood and had to return to being laymen, the most serious punishment in Buddhism. Other disciples suggested that Uppalavanna also deserved to be expelled from the priesthood because she, too, committed adultery.

Shakyamuni Buddha softly asked Uppalavanna, "Did you feel any pleasure when the men raped you?" Uppalavanna answered, "I felt no pleasure." Then, Shakyamuni replied, "You did no wrong. Devote yourself to your spiritual training like before." She was not punished for violating the precepts. Uppalavanna continued to devote herself to her spiritual training and became a well-known Buddhist nun who demonstrated the qualities of six divine supernatural powers.

Next, Doman told Taeko about another famous female disciple in the history of Buddhism: Ambapali, a former high-class prostitute. Said to be the most beautiful woman in India, Ambapali was a rich prostitute who dealt only with politicians and high-ranking bureaucrats in today's terms, but she felt the impermanence of the world and renounced the world to become a nun. She was a single mother like we often see today, and she had a son whose father was unknown. She made her son a monk. Ambapali herself donated the Ambapali Garden to Buddha's Order and became a nun. Shakyamuni Buddha accepted her donation and her entering the priesthood, and there is even a dialogue between Ambapali and Shakyamuni recorded in a sutra. Doman commented that St. Agnes' case was rather similar to that of Uppalavanna.

There is a theory in Christianity that Mary Magdalene, a prostitute, was the lover of Jesus Christ. The theory goes that she was virtually his wife. St. Peter, the first pope, did not think well of this. Another theory goes that Judas' true motive behind his betrayal was his jealousy toward Mary Magdalene's devotion to Jesus. When Magdalene poured expensive scented oil on her long hair and used it to wipe Jesus' feet, Judas became set on betraying Jesus. That was the moment the devil entered Judas, or so it is said. Mary Magdalene became a saint who even had a church built in veneration of her.

"Therefore," said Doman, "I believe what is most important is the purity of the mind and the devotion to God and Buddha." That was Doman's theory.

Agnes felt ever so slightly forgiven by Buddha and Christ. *I may still have a chance to get back on my feet*, she thought.

20.

Detective Noyama worked day and night until the whereabouts of Michio Taneda, the freelance writer, became clearer. He was spotted at several Internet cafés.

They also learned that Michio Taneda had finally reached one of the four men who assaulted his daughter. Goro Ichikawa was a henchman of Daisaku Sato, an assistant to the deputy leader of the Motoyama Crime Family based in Shinagawa. Ichikawa was mainly in charge of collecting protection money from the gang-affiliated sex-industry shops. At times, he was also involved in a business of trafficking women in need of money to those shops.

Agnes' father Taneda tried to write a detailed story on the Motoyama Family, and he dug too far… One rainy day, he stopped by Petite Cinderella, one of the hostess bars under the protection of the gang, and went missing after that. Detective Noyama consulted Yamasaki and the others. If they were to confront the gang, they would have to partner with the Organized Crime Control Bureau and set up a joint investigation meeting. But Team Yamasaki was still handling unresolved cases.

"For now, Team Yamasaki will work by ourselves for one week," Chief Yamasaki decided. He thought that four detectives were enough to rescue the father.

However, Agnes, a.k.a. Taeko Taneda, overheard about her father when Noyama blurted out that he had succeeded in tracing her father's whereabouts. She wasn't confirmed as a suspect yet, so she was voluntarily under the protection of Team Yamasaki as both an important witness and a collaborator.

"If you're going to find my father, please let me go with you. You'll need me," Agnes asked them.

"But you might be put in danger," Yamasaki said.

"I've caused my family years of stress. Besides, all my memory might return once I see my father."

Agnes' strong request convinced them to bring her under the condition that Doman and Yuri would protect Agnes, while Yamasaki and Noyama would take the lead and step up in any dangerous situations if necessary.

Then, all of a sudden, Agnes opened her mouth to speak: "My father is locked up in a warehouse of a company called Motoyama Real Estate." She had requested to come along because she wanted to use her supernatural powers for the investigation.

Yuri and Agnes stayed in the car while the three men stepped into the Motoyama Real Estate building. After a while, they heard a gunshot.

"No worries," Yuri said. "Mr. Yamasaki is the best shooter we have in our division. Mr. Noyama is Nagoya's ace in judo and also his skills in arresting criminals. Doman has a third-degree black belt in karate. They can easily deal with four or five members of the gang."

"No, it's not good. One guy has a machine gun. Our three guys will be in danger as it is. Trust me. Ms. Yuri, please take me to them," Agnes pleaded.

"Fine, I guess I have no choice. You can use your supernatural powers from a distance, but leave the combat up to us, alright?" Okada said.

The two women climbed up the stairs and stepped onto Motoyama Family's turf. The security was tighter than they had thought, which meant that Michio Taneda was inside.

Two members of the gang were already knocked out and covered in blood. They were shot in a way that wasn't fatal. Yamasaki must've shot them. There were also two men beaten on the ground. Detective Noyama must've used his judo techniques. Yet there were six guys left. It seemed that the Motoyama Family boss, Torazo Motoyama, was here in the back room.

There was one guy with a machine gun, one with a katana, one with a pistol, and others with wooden swords.

Team Yamasaki seemed to be struggling with the machine gun and Japanese sword. Yamasaki spilled, "Should I have called the Special Assault Team after all?"

Agnes walked toward the gang without flinching.

"Are you insane?!" It was not the detectives who shouted this but the guys from the Motoyama Family.

First, the Japanese swordsman rushed toward Agnes to slash her, but this time Agnes broke the katana into five pieces.

Next, the man with the machine gun shot a volley of bullets, all of which curved to hit the walls, ceiling, and windows. Agnes grabbed the upper receiver of the man's machine gun and twisted it like a piece of soft candy.

Seeing this, the gang surrendered. The man holding the pistol and the men holding wooden swords dropped their weapons. They were immediately handcuffed.

Agnes kicked open the back room. She twisted the gang boss' arms and pushed his head up toward the ceiling, making him faint.

Her father, Michio Taneda, was locked up in a warehouse in the back.

"Dad, I'm sorry," Agnes said as she took off the gag and untied his rope. The other four arrested the gang members and called for additional police cars and ambulances.

The father needed hospitalization for a while. The four members of Team Yamasaki were totally taken aback by Agnes' psychic powers. It was just as Yuri Okada had testified.

It appeared as though the case had moved forward, but things weren't that simple. Across the building, a man was watching the entire turn of events from beginning to end through a window. It was Mitsuo Maejima from the Men in Black Japan.

.ied a video of Agnes and sent it over
.nistry of Defense.

. nat day, they confirmed that one of the gang
members once assaulted Agnes in Nagoya. Agnes,
on the other hand, did not return to her shelter in
Daikanyama.

In fact, the agents from MIBJ had taken her away
from the First Criminal Investigation Division.

The story was now entering the next stage.

21.

The black bulletproof car drove into the Self-Defense Forces' Camp Ichigaya instead of the Ministry of Defense. They had escaped from several
police cars that were chasing them with flashing
red lights. The sky was already turning dark.

"Even the cops can't enter a Self-Defense
Forces' camp without permission. I'll ask you to
cooperate with us here," Maejima said.

"I still have unfinished business with everyone
from the division," Agnes said. "I also need to meet
my family. I could be a criminal, so I may have to
atone for my sins."

She wasn't sure how she had walked through
the camp building until she reached a distinctive
room.

She was escorted into a 350-sq. ft. room, where
Director General Hideki Takahashi, captain of the
MIBJ, was awaiting her arrival.

"I'm sorry for our aggressive approach. Right now, Japan is in the midst of a crisis. It isn't a time to be chasing murder cases. I'm the director general of the Special Mission Intelligence Bureau that belongs to the Ministry of Defense. We already know of your special powers," Takahashi said.

Another man stepped forward. It was Takao Hirose, chief of staff of the Air Self-Defense Force.

"St. Agnes," he called her by her holy name. "Secret agents from the CIA and KGB, as well as North Korea and China, are infiltrating Japan as spies. Based on our research, we know that one of our enemy spies has supernatural powers and can replicate the special abilities of other psychics. That's why we can't allow your powers to be seen outside of this Self-Defense Forces base."

Just then, an ICBM was launched from North Korea on a lofted trajectory, which would rise to an altitude of 3,700 miles before falling. It hit near the area where the PAC-3 missiles were installed in

Camp Ichigaya. Fortunately—though this may not be appropriate commentary—it was not a nuclear missile.

But there was fire everywhere inside the base.

It was a state of emergency. The gates were opened, and fire engines and ambulances rushed in one after another.

In one of the ambulances, riding undercover, were Yamasaki and the other three.

They had received a covert mission from the superintendent general: "Retrieve Taeko Taneda from the Ministry of Defense." The order was also approved by the commissioner general of the National Police Agency.

"They took advantage of our chaos after the Motoyama Family incident and took her away, claiming themselves to be a high-ranking authority of the Ministry of Defense," said Yamasaki. "But since the superintendent general of the Tokyo Metropolitan Police Department ordered us to take her back, we'll fulfill our duty even by fighting the Self-Defense Forces."

"That's right! Let's make it happen," the other three said.

They ran through the flames, each wearing a helmet and a white coat and carrying a handgun in their pockets. Somehow, Detective Doman clearly heard Agnes' telepathic voice and they easily located the room she was in.

They kicked the door open. The officials from both the Ministry of Defense and the Self-Defense Forces were bewildered by the sight of the police in white coats and helmets.

Detective Noyama took this opportunity to throw Director General Takahashi on the ground and handcuff him. Detective Okada knocked down Mitsuo Maejima with a whirling kick, and she put handcuffs on him as she straddled him. Yamasaki hit the chief of staff of the Air Self-Defense Force on the head with an extendable baton, immediately causing him to lose consciousness. The other two were handcuffed as well.

The four members of Team Yamasaki and Agnes breathed a sigh of relief.

"Alright, let's get out of here," Yamasaki said.

Just then, members of the Self-Defense Forces poured in wearing gas masks and bulletproof vests. They fired tear gas bullets. Team Yamasaki couldn't move. The Self-Defense Forces thought Yamasaki and the others were secret agents of enemy countries. They never imagined that police officers would attack high-ranking officials of the Ministry of Defense and the Self-Defense Forces. The rioting of the detectives had been caught on surveillance cameras.

A total of 100 bullets were shot from two machine guns. Doman Yogiashi was shot in his left eye and fell down. Mitsuru Noyama was shot twice in his right thigh, and he, too, fell down.

Chief Yamasaki was holding up his police badge in his right hand when he was shot 10 times at various points on his body. He died instantly.

Just then, Agnes, who was crouched, stood up. She held out her right hand toward five bullets that were flying toward Detective Yuri Okada and shifted the bullets' trajectory away.

At that moment, Yuri Okada screamed, "We're from the Tokyo Metropolitan Police Department, First Criminal Investigation Division!" She landed flying kicks on the two officers with machine guns, high kicks that collided with their faces.

At that moment, a bullet that was aimed at Yuri flew under her waist and penetrated the chest of St. Agnes, a.k.a. Taeko Taneda. Even Agnes couldn't see the bullet coming.

Detective Yuri Okada knocked out the two men wielding machine guns and ran over to Agnes. Her chest was stained with blood.

"You can't die. You can't die," Yuri repeated as she ripped Agnes' clothes to examine the wound on her chest. There was a black cross-shaped bruise between her breasts.

A bullet had hit the point of intersection of the cross and blood was streaming out. The bullet with which Agnes was shot moved in a diverted direction and came out of her body, falling to the right.

"Agnes, you'll be saved." Yuri was relieved.

"Ms. Yuri, you can't look at the cross," said Agnes.

"What? Is that right?"

Those were Yuri's last words. Her eyes rolled back and she foamed at the mouth, falling to the left.

Agnes knew that she, too, would soon die. She was losing too much blood.

"I was going to save Ms. Yuri." Saying so, she fell to the floor with her stiffened neck rolling over to the side.

This incident was a fight between the National Police Agency and both the Ministry of Defense and the Self-Defense Forces, so it had to be kept secret from the media and the public.

The media simply reported that many people were killed by an ICBM from North Korea.

The prime minister was in hiding, so Chief Cabinet Secretary Koichi Mamiya held a press conference in the former's absence.

"We strongly protest against North Korea's violent behavior. The Japanese government will make an official decision at the next Diet meeting to develop a preemptive long-range missile within a year," Mamiya said.

Mamiya did not yet know that 50 missiles had been launched from Fujian Province in China toward Taiwan; nor did he know that the Chinese army had reached Senkaku Islands and built an anti-aircraft, anti-ship missile base overnight.

He also did not know that Russian Air Force bombers from the Northern Territories were presently bombing Sapporo.

The Japanese government abruptly and effectively stopped functioning upon receiving simultaneous blows from three neighboring countries—North Korea, Russia, and China.

Around the same time, U.S. President Obamiden was at a golf course, about to putt his ball into the ninth hole. He burst into pieces after being shot by small missiles from 50 drones.

That was around the time that Russia had shot ICBMs toward the U.K., Germany, and France.

The world became chaotic without a leader.

Meanwhile, the souls of St. Agnes and Yuri Okada were soaring toward heaven.

At Master's Holy Temple of Happy Science, Master Ryuho Okawa muttered under his breath.

"Agnes is dead. To die at such a young age, it was unfortunate, Seraph."

Tokyo was filled with deep silence.

There was fire everywhere, but all appeared to be a silent world.

END of the story.

22.

The following was discovered after the end of the story. A last will and testament by Agnes, addressed to her father, was found in a desk drawer of the room St. Agnes had used as a shelter at the dormitory of the Bank of Japan in Daikanyama.

Last Will: Dear Father, who raised me with love:

After all you have done to raise me, with so much affection for 18 years, I can only tell you my feelings in such a way. You can laugh at your poor daughter if you choose to.

I will do anything I can to find you, Father. I'm sure I will succeed. But if you're reading this, it means that I am no longer a resident of this world.

I was caught up in several incidents in the past, and I will continue to be caught up in more. This is my destiny, and with the end of my destiny comes the end of my power and my mission.

Let me briefly explain to you what happened.

That day, in my senior year of high school, I saw a young man with an injured leg. I let him use my shoulder to lean on, and I walked him to his house nearby. Rain was starting to drizzle. Once I entered an open garage door and dropped him off, I realized that it was an empty house and that I was caught in a trap by four young men. They shut the garage door, and the four of them assaulted me one by one. I was raped, and I lost my virginity. It hurt, I was embarrassed, and I almost wanted to commit suicide. They let me go after 30 minutes or so. I ran up a sloped street, drenched, wearing only a cloth of chemise. I was a ball of shame. There was a roar of thunder, and as heavy rain poured on me, I prayed to God. "Please kill those four men." At that moment, an old cherry tree nearby was struck by lightning, and I lost consciousness. Three days later, I was being taken care of at a nunnery of a church. Perhaps from severe shock, I lost all my memory. The nunnery gave me the holy name "Agnes," and for several years, I helped out by selling the Bible, making cookies to raise donations, and helping out with bazaar events. One night, Jesus stood by my bedside and said, "Agnes, be born again. I shall bear you a sacred mark of the cross like the Stigma. That natural bruise you have on your chest will turn into the shape of a cross, and you will live on my behalf. You will never again suffer from assault, but in return, you must live your life as a nun without ever marrying because whoever sees the cross on your white breasts is bound to die. You must not mistake it for the power of the devil. It is to convey my true feelings to the modern people of this world, the feelings of the person who was crucified on the cross and died for the salvation of humankind. The cross symbolizes 'death and resurrection.'"

Thereafter, I performed several miracles in Nagoya, but His Excellency Archbishop of Tokyo Ignatius summoned me out of suspicion. He wanted to determine if it was the power of the devil or the power of God.

I went all the way to Tokyo Station, but I decided to escape at the last minute. I moved around different parks. During that time, I was almost raped again by men in Arisugawa Park, Odaiba, and Yoyogi Park.

But as soon as they exposed my breasts and saw the Stigma, they all rolled their eyes back and foamed at their mouths. They all died.

As a result, I was chased by the members of the First Criminal Investigation Division on suspicion of a serial killing. In the meantime, I went into hiding by working at a hostess bar and a flower shop. But my ability to perform miracles was leaked to the MIBJ (Men in Black Japan) of the Ministry of Defense, and they are now thinking of using me as a tool to find undercover spies from foreign countries. In any case, my mission does not extend as far as saving this country, so I think I'll end up dying in battle. The people from MIBJ probably want to use my ability to foresee the future and to gain remote killing powers.

But I intend to die in faith as a nun.

Father, you raised me with great care, but please forgive your daughter for turning into an X-MEN-like monster. Some people will die in the near future. I can't save this country.

There is a real Savior. I'm just His precursor.

Finally, I truly wish for mother and brother to live happily as well.

I lived at the mercy of destiny, but it'd be my greatest pleasure to at least tell you that God is alive.

(St. Agnes)

The letter ended there.

St. Agnes has yet to know that she is one of the four Seraphim, the highest rank angels.

Her true work may start extensively once she returns to heaven.

A highest ranked angel was born in this country of Japan that is heading toward destruction. She displayed her supernatural powers after experiencing sins and forgiveness, and she died young. There is no doubt that she was born to cause a stir in a world that had become too materialistic. It was also the guidance of Jesus to the church that no longer believes in miracles.

I hope you feel the Light in the midst of adversity.

THE END

ABOUT THE AUTHOR

Founder and CEO of Happy Science Group.

Ryuho Okawa was born on July 7th 1956, in Tokushima, Japan. After graduating from the University of Tokyo with a law degree, he joined a Tokyo-based trading house. While working at its New York headquarters, he studied international finance at the Graduate Center of the City University of New York. In 1981, he attained Great Enlightenment and became aware that he is El Cantare with a mission to bring salvation to all humankind.

In 1986, he established Happy Science. It now has members in over 165 countries across the world, with more than 700 branches and temples as well as 10,000 missionary houses around the world.

He has given over 3,400 lectures (of which more than 150 are in English) and published over 3,000 books (of which more than 600 are Spiritual Interview Series), and many are translated into 40 languages. Along with *The Laws of the Sun* and *The Laws Of Messiah*, many of the books have become best sellers or million sellers. To date, Happy Science has produced 25 movies. The original story and original concept were given by the Executive Producer Ryuho Okawa. He has also composed music and written lyrics of over 450 pieces.

Moreover, he is the Founder of Happy Science University and Happy Science Academy (Junior and Senior High School), Founder and President of the Happiness Realization Party, Founder and Honorary Headmaster of Happy Science Institute of Government and Management, Founder of IRH Press Co., Ltd., and the Chairperson of NEW STAR PRODUCTION Co., Ltd. and ARI Production Co., Ltd.

WHAT IS EL CANTARE?

El Cantare means "the Light of the Earth," and is the Supreme God of the Earth who has been guiding humankind since the beginning of Genesis. He is whom Jesus called Father and Muhammad called Allah, and is *Ame-no-Mioya-Gami*, Japanese Father God. Different parts of El Cantare's core consciousness have descended to Earth in the past, once as Alpha and another as Elohim. His branch spirits, such as Shakyamuni Buddha and Hermes, have descended to Earth many times and helped to flourish many civilizations. To unite various religions and to integrate various fields of study in order to build a new civilization on Earth, a part of the core consciousness has descended to Earth as Master Ryuho Okawa.

Alpha is a part of the core consciousness of El Cantare who descended to Earth around 330 million years ago. Alpha preached Earth's Truths to harmonize and unify Earth-born humans and space people who came from other planets.

Elohim is a part of El Cantare's core consciousness who descended to Earth around 150 million years ago. He gave wisdom, mainly on the differences of light and darkness, good and evil.

Ame-no-Mioya-Gami (Japanese Father God) is the Creator God and the Father God who appears in the ancient literature, *Hotsuma Tsutae*. It is believed that He descended on the foothills of Mt. Fuji about 30,000 years ago and built the Fuji dynasty, which is the root of the Japanese civilization. With justice as the central pillar, Ame-no-Mioya-Gami's teachings spread to ancient civilizations of other countries in the world.

Shakyamuni Buddha was born as a prince into the Shakya Clan in India around 2,600 years ago. When he was 29 years old, he renounced the world and sought enlightenment. He later attained Great Enlightenment and founded Buddhism.

Hermes is one of the 12 Olympian gods in Greek mythology, but the spiritual Truth is that he taught the teachings of love and progress around 4,300 years ago that became the origin of the current Western civilization. He is a hero that truly existed.

Ophealis was born in Greece around 6,500 years ago and was the leader who took an expedition to as far as Egypt. He is the God of miracles, prosperity, and arts, and is known as Osiris in the Egyptian mythology.

Rient Arl Croud was born as a king of the ancient Incan Empire around 7,000 years ago and taught about the mysteries of the mind. In the heavenly world, he is responsible for the interactions that take place between various planets.

Thoth was an almighty leader who built the golden age of the Atlantic civilization around 12,000 years ago. In the Egyptian mythology, he is known as god Thoth.

Ra Mu was a leader who built the golden age of the civilization of Mu around 17,000 years ago. As a religious leader and a politician, he ruled by uniting religion and politics.

The Unknown Stigma Series

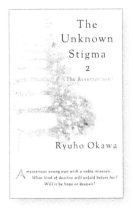

The Unknown Stigma 2
\<The Resurrection>

Paperback • 176 pages • $16.95
ISBN: 979-8-88737-014-9 (Jun. 30, 2022)

A sequel to *The Unknown Stigma 1 \<The Mystery>* by Ryuho Okawa. After an extraordinary spiritual experience, a young, mysterious Catholic nun is now endowed with a new, noble mission. What kind of destiny will she face? Will it be hope or despair that awaits her? The story develops into a turn of events that no one could ever have anticipated. Are you ready to embrace its shocking ending?

Coming in July 2022

The Unknown Stigma 3
\<The Universe>

Paperback • 194 pages • $16.95
ISBN: 979-8-88737-020-0

In this astonishing sequel to the first two installments of *The Unknown Stigma*, the protagonist journeys through the universe and encounters a mystical world unknown to humankind. Discover what awaits her beyond this mysterious world.

Coming in August 2022

THE REBIRTH OF BUDDHA

MY ETERNAL DISCIPLES,
HEAR MY WORDS

Hardcover • 280 pages • $17.95
ISBN: 978-1-942125-95-2

These are the messages of Buddha who has returned to this modern age as promised to His eternal beloved disciples. They are in simple words and poetic style, yet contain profound messages. Once you start reading these passages, your soul will be replenished as the plant absorbs the water, and you will remember why you chose this era to be born into with Buddha. Listen to the voices of your Eternal Master and awaken to your calling.

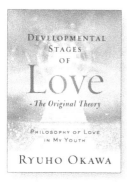

Published on June 15, 2022

DEVELOPMENTAL STAGES OF LOVE
- THE ORIGINAL THEORY

PHILOSOPHY OF LOVE IN MY YOUTH

Hardcover • 200 pages • $17.95
ISBN: 978-1-942125-94-5

This book is about author Ryuho Okawa's original philosophy of love which serves as the foundation of love in the chapter three of *The Laws of the Sun*. It consists of series of short essays authored during his age of 25 through 28 while he was working as a young promising business elite at an international trading company after attaining the Great Enlightenment in 1981. The developmental stages of love unites love and enlightenment, West and East, and bridges Christianity and Buddhism.

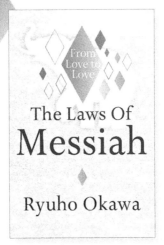

The Laws Of Messiah
From Love to Love

Paperback • 248 pages • $16.95
ISBN: 978-1-942125-90-7 (Jan. 31, 2022)

"What is Messiah?" This book carries an important message of love and guidance to people living now from the Modern-Day Messiah or the Modern-Day Savior. It also reveals the secret of Shambhala, the spiritual center of Earth, as well as the truth that this spiritual center is currently in danger of perishing and what we can do to protect this sacred place.

Love your Lord God. Know that those who don't know love don't know God. Discover the true love of God and the ideal practice of faith. This book teaches the most important element we must not lose sight of as we go through our soul training on this planet Earth.

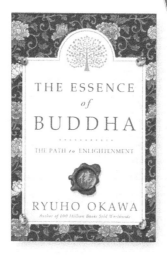

BESTSELLING BUDDHIST TITLE

THE ESSENCE OF BUDDHA

THE PATH TO ENLIGHTENMENT

Paperback • 208 pages • $14.95
ISBN: 978-1-942125-06-8 (Oct.1, 2016)

In this book, Ryuho Okawa imparts in simple and accessible language his wisdom about the essence of Shakyamuni Buddha's philosophy of life and enlightenment–teachings that have been inspiring people all over the world for over 2,500 years. By offering a new perspective on core Buddhist thoughts that have long been cloaked in mystique, Okawa brings these teachings to life for modern people. *The Essence of Buddha* distills a way of life that anyone can practice to achieve a life of self-growth, compassionate living, and true happiness.

THE TRILOGY

The first three volumes of the Laws Series, *The Laws of the Sun*, *The Golden Laws*, and *The Nine Dimensions* make a trilogy that completes the basic framework of the teachings of God's Truths. *The Laws of the Sun* discusses the structure of God's Laws, *The Golden Laws* expounds on the doctrine of time, and *The Nine Dimensions* reveals the nature of space.

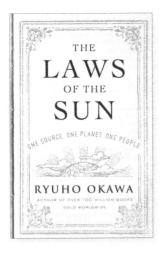

THE LAWS OF THE SUN

ONE SOURCE, ONE PLANET,
ONE PEOPLE

Paperback • 288 pages • $15.95
ISBN: 978-1-942125-43-3 (Oct. 15, 2018)

IMAGINE IF YOU COULD ASK GOD why He created this world and what spiritual laws He used to shape us—and everything around us. If we could understand His designs and intentions, we could discover what our goals in life should be and whether our actions move us closer to those goals or farther away.

At a young age, a spiritual calling prompted Ryuho Okawa to outline what he innately understood to be universal truths for all humankind. In *The Laws of the Sun*, Okawa outlines these laws of the universe and provides a road map for living one's life with greater purpose and meaning.

In this powerful book, Ryuho Okawa reveals the transcendent nature of consciousness and the secrets of our multidimensional universe and our place in it. By understanding the different stages of love and following the Buddhist Eightfold Path, he believes we can speed up our eternal process of development. *The Laws of the Sun* shows the way to realize true happiness—a happiness that continues from this world through the other.

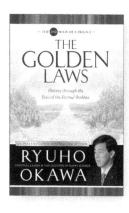

THE GOLDEN LAWS
HISTORY THROUGH THE EYES OF THE ETERNAL BUDDHA

E-book • 201 pages • $13.99
ISBN: 978-1-941779-82-8

Throughout history, Great Guiding Spirits have been present on Earth in both the East and the West at crucial points in human history to further our spiritual development. *The Golden Laws* reveals how Divine Plan has been unfolding on Earth, and outlines 5,000 years of the secret history of humankind. Once we understand the true course of history, through past, present and into the future, we cannot help but become aware of the significance of our spiritual mission in the present age.

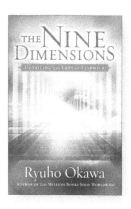

THE NINE DIMENSIONS
UNVEILING THE LAWS OF ETERNITY

Paperback • 168 pages • $15.95
ISBN: 978-0-982698-56-3 (Feb. 16, 2012)

This book is a window into the mind of our loving God, who designed this world and the vast, wondrous world of our afterlife as a school with many levels through which our souls learn and grow. When the religions and cultures of the world discover the truth of their common spiritual origin, they will be inspired to accept their differences, come together under faith in God, and build an era of harmony and peaceful progress on Earth.

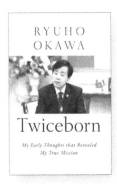

TWICEBORN

MY EARLY THOUGHTS THAT REVEALED
MY TRUE MISSION

Hardcover • 206 pages • $19.95
ISBN: 978-1-942125-74-7 (Oct. 7, 2020)

This semi-autobiography of Ryuho Okawa reveals the origins of his thoughts and how he made up his mind to establish Happy Science to spread the Truth to the world. It also contains the very first grand lecture where he declared himself as El Cantare. The timeless wisdom in *Twiceborn* will surely inspire you and help you fulfill your mission in this lifetime.

THE NEW RESURRECTION

MY MIRACULOUS STORY OF
OVERCOMING ILLNESS AND DEATH

Hardcover • 224 pages • $19.95
ISBN: 978-1-942125-64-8 (Feb. 26, 2020)

The New Resurrection is an autobiographical account of an astonishing miracle experienced by author Ryuho Okawa in 2004. This event was adapted into the feature-length film *Immortal Hero*. Today, Okawa lives each day with the readiness to die for the Truth and has dedicated his life to selflessly guiding faith seekers towards spiritual development and happiness.

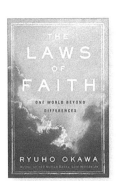

THE LAWS OF FAITH

ONE WORLD BEYOND DIFFERENCES

Paperback • 208 pages • $15.95
ISBN: 978-1-942125-34-1 (Mar. 31, 2018)

Ryuho Okawa preaches at the core of a new universal religion from various angles while integrating logical and spiritual viewpoints in mind with current world situations. This book offers us the key to accept diversities beyond differences to create a world filled with peace and prosperity.

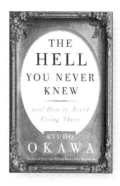

THE HELL YOU NEVER KNEW

AND HOW TO AVOID GOING THERE

Paperback • 192 pages • $15.95
ISBN: 978-1-942125-52-5 (Jul. 15, 2019)

From ancient times, people have been warned of the danger of falling to Hell. But does the world of Hell truly exist? If it does, what kind of people would go there? Through his spiritual abilities, Ryuho Okawa found out that Hell is only a small part of the vast Spirit World, yet more than half of the people today go there after they die.

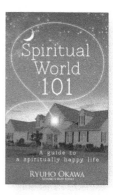

SPIRITUAL WORLD 101

A GUIDE TO A SPIRITUALLY HAPPY LIFE

Paperback • $14.95 • ISBN: 978-1-941779-43-9
E-book • $13.99 • ISBN: 978-1-941779-45-3

This book is a spiritual guidebook that will answer all your questions about the spiritual world,with illustrations and diagrams explaining about your guardian spirit and the secrets of God and Buddha. By reading this book, you will be able to understand the true meaning of life and find happiness in everyday life.

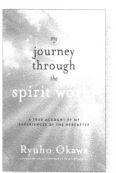

MY JOURNEY THROUGH THE SPIRIT WORLD

A TRUE ACCOUNT OF MY EXPERIENCES OF THE HEREAFTER

Paperback • 224 pages • $15.95
ISBN: 978-1-942125-41-9 (Jul. 25, 2018)

What happens when we die? Do heaven and hell really exist? This book reveals surprising facts such as that we visit the spirit world during sleep and that people continue to live in the same lifestyle as they did in this world. This unique and authentic guide to the spirit world will awaken us to the truth of life and death, and show us how we can return to a bright world of heaven.

RECENT SPIRITUAL MESSAGES

SPIRITUAL MESSAGES FROM YAIDRON
SAVE THE WORLD FROM
DESTRUCTION

Paperback • $11.95 • ISBN: 978-1-943928-23-1
E-book • $10.99 • ISBN: 978-1-943928-25-5

In this book, Yaidron explains what was going on behind the military coup in Myanmar and Taliban's control over Afghanistan. He also warns of the imminent danger approaching Taiwan. What is now going on is a battle between democratic values and the communist one-party control. How to overcome this battle and create peace on Earth depends on the faith and righteous actions of each one of us.

THE DESCENT OF JAPANESE
FATHER GOD AME-NO-MIOYA-GAMI

THE "GOD OF CREATION" IN THE ANCIENT DOCUMENT HOTSUMA TSUTAE

Paperback • $14.95 • ISBN: 978-1-943928-35-4
E-book • $13.99 • ISBN: 978-1-943928-31-6

By reading this book, you can find the origin of bushido (samurai spirit) and understand how the ancient Japanese civilization influenced other countries. Now that the world is in confusion, Japan is expected to awaken to its true origin and courageously rise to bring justice to the world.

SPIRITUAL MESSAGES FROM METATRON
LIGHT IN THE TIMES OF CRISIS

Paperback • 146 pages • $11.95
ISBN: 978-1-943928-19-4 (Nov. 4, 2021)

Metatron is one of the highest-ranking angels (seraphim) in Judaism and Christianity, and also one of the saviors of universe who has guided the civilizations of many planets including Earth, under the guidance of Lord God. Such savior has sent a message upon seeing the crisis of Earth. You will also learn about the truth behind the coronavirus pandemic, the unimaginable extent of China's desire, the danger of appeasement policy toward China, and the secret of Metatron.

OTHER RECOMMENDED TITLES

THE LAWS OF SECRET
Awaken to This New World and Change Your Life

THE MYSTICAL LAWS
Going Beyond the Dimensional Boundaries

THE LAWS OF MISSION
Essential Truths for Spiritual Awakening in a Secular Age

THE UNHAPPINESS SYNDROME
28 Habits of Unhappy People (and How to Change Them)

HEALING FROM WITHIN
Life-Changing Keys to Calm, Spiritual, and Healthy Living

HEALING POWER
The True Mechanism of Mind and Illness

THE POSSESSION
Know the Ghost Condition and
Overcome Negative Spiritual Influence

BASICS OF EXORCISM
How to Protect You and Your Family from Evil Spirits

THE REAL EXORCIST
Attain Wisdom to Conquer Evil

For a complete list of books, visit okawabooks.com

MUSIC BY RYUHO OKAWA

El Cantare Ryuho Okawa Original Songs

A song celebrating Lord God

A song celebrating Lord God,
the God of the Earth,
who is beyond a prophet.

DVD
CD

The Water Revolution

English and Chinese version

For the truth and happiness of
the 1.4 billion people in China
who have no freedom. Love,
justice, and sacred rage of God
are on this melody that will
give you courage to fight to
bring peace.

DVD

CD

Search on YouTube

the water revolution for a short ad!

Listen now today!

 Download from
Spotify iTunes Amazon

DVD, CD available at amazon.com,
and Happy Science locations worldwide

With Savior *English version*

This is the message of hope to the modern people who are living in the midst of the Coronavirus pandemic, natural disasters, economic depression, and other various crises.

Search on YouTube

with savior for a short ad!

The Thunder
a composition for repelling the Coronavirus

We have been granted this music from our Lord. It will repel away the novel Coronavirus originated in China. Experience this magnificent powerful music.

Search on YouTube

the thunder composition

for a short ad!

The Exorcism
prayer music for repelling Lost Spirits

Feel the divine vibrations of this Japanese and Western exorcising symphony to banish all evil possessions you suffer from and to purify your space!

Search on YouTube

the exorcism repelling

for a short ad!

Listen now today!

 Download from
Spotify iTunes Amazon

DVD, CD available at amazon.com, and Happy Science locations worldwide

ABOUT HAPPY SCIENCE

Happy Science is a global movement that empowers individuals to find purpose and spiritual happiness and to share that happiness with their families, societies, and the world. With more than 12 million members around the world, Happy Science aims to increase awareness of spiritual truths and expand our capacity for love, compassion, and joy so that together we can create the kind of world we all wish to live in.

Activities at Happy Science are based on the Principle of Happiness (Love, Wisdom, Self-Reflection, and Progress). This principle embraces worldwide philosophies and beliefs, transcending boundaries of culture and religions.

Love teaches us to give ourselves freely without expecting anything in return; it encompasses giving, nurturing, and forgiving.

Wisdom leads us to the insights of spiritual truths, and opens us to the true meaning of life and the will of God (the universe, the highest power, Buddha).

Self-Reflection brings a mindful, nonjudgmental lens to our thoughts and actions to help us find our truest selves—the essence of our souls—and deepen our connection to the highest power. It helps us attain a clean and peaceful mind and leads us to the right life path.

Progress emphasizes the positive, dynamic aspects of our spiritual growth—actions we can take to manifest and spread happiness around the world. It's a path that not only expands our soul growth, but also furthers the collective potential of the world we live in.

PROGRAMS AND EVENTS

The doors of Happy Science are open to all. We offer a variety of programs and events, including self-exploration and self-growth programs, spiritual seminars, meditation and contemplation sessions, study groups, and book events.

Our programs are designed to:
* Deepen your understanding of your purpose and meaning in life
* Improve your relationships and increase your capacity to love unconditionally
* Attain peace of mind, decrease anxiety and stress, and feel positive
* Gain deeper insights and a broader perspective on the world
* Learn how to overcome life's challenges
    ... and much more.

For more information, visit <u>happy-science.org</u>.

CONTACT INFORMATION

Happy Science is a worldwide organization with branches and temples around the globe. For a comprehensive list, visit the worldwide directory at *happy-science.org*. The following are some of the many Happy Science locations:

UNITED STATES AND CANADA

New York
79 Franklin St., New York, NY 10013, USA
Phone: 1-212-343-7972
Fax: 1-212-343-7973
Email: ny@happy-science.org
Website: happyscience-usa.org

New Jersey
66 Hudson St., #2R, Hoboken, NJ 07030, USA
Phone: 1-201-313-0127
Email: nj@happy-science.org
Website: happyscience-usa.org

Chicago
2300 Barrington Rd., Suite #400,
Hoffman Estates, IL 60169, USA
Phone: 1-630-937-3077
Email: chicago@happy-science.org
Website: happyscience-usa.org

Florida
5208 8th St., Zephyrhills, FL 33542, USA
Phone: 1-813-715-0000
Fax: 1-813-715-0010
Email: florida@happy-science.org
Website: happyscience-usa.org

Atlanta
1874 Piedmont Ave., NE Suite 360-C
Atlanta, GA 30324, USA
Phone: 1-404-892-7770
Email: atlanta@happy-science.org
Website: happyscience-usa.org

San Francisco
525 Clinton St.
Redwood City, CA 94062, USA
Phone & Fax: 1-650-363-2777
Email: sf@happy-science.org
Website: happyscience-usa.org

Los Angeles
1590 E. Del Mar Blvd., Pasadena, CA
91106, USA
Phone: 1-626-395-7775
Fax: 1-626-395-7776
Email: la@happy-science.org
Website: happyscience-usa.org

Orange County
16541 Gothard St. Suite 104
Huntington Beach, CA 92647
Phone: 1-714-659-1501
Email: oc@happy-science.org
Website: happyscience-usa.org

San Diego
7841 Balboa Ave. Suite #202
San Diego, CA 92111, USA
Phone: 1-626-395-7775
Fax: 1-626-395-7776
E-mail: sandiego@happy-science.org
Website: happyscience-usa.org

Hawaii
Phone: 1-808-591-9772
Fax: 1-808-591-9776
Email: hi@happy-science.org
Website: happyscience-usa.org

Kauai
3343 Kanakolu Street, Suite 5
Lihue, HI 96766, USA
Phone: 1-808-822-7007
Fax: 1-808-822-6007
Email: kauai-hi@happy-science.org
Website: happyscience-usa.org

Toronto

845 The Queensway
Etobicoke, ON M8Z 1N6, Canada
Phone: 1-416-901-3747
Email: toronto@happy-science.org
Website: happy-science.ca

Vancouver

#201-2607 East 49th Avenue,
Vancouver, BC, V5S 1J9, Canada
Phone: 1-604-437-7735
Fax: 1-604-437-7764
Email: vancouver@happy-science.org
Website: happy-science.ca

INTERNATIONAL

Tokyo

1-6-7 Togoshi, Shinagawa,
Tokyo, 142-0041, Japan
Phone: 81-3-6384-5770
Fax: 81-3-6384-5776
Email: tokyo@happy-science.org
Website: happy-science.org

Seoul

74, Sadang-ro 27-gil,
Dongjak-gu, Seoul, Korea
Phone: 82-2-3478-8777
Fax: 82-2-3478-9777
Email: korea@happy-science.org
Website: happyscience-korea.org

London

3 Margaret St.
London, W1W 8RE United Kingdom
Phone: 44-20-7323-9255
Fax: 44-20-7323-9344
Email: eu@happy-science.org
Website: www.happyscience-uk.org

Taipei

No. 89, Lane 155, Dunhua N. Road,
Songshan District, Taipei City 105, Taiwan
Phone: 886-2-2719-9377
Fax: 886-2-2719-5570
Email: taiwan@happy-science.org
Website: happyscience-tw.org

Sydney

516 Pacific Highway, Lane Cove North,
2066 NSW, Australia
Phone: 61-2-9411-2877
Fax: 61-2-9411-2822
Email: sydney@happy-science.org

Kuala Lumpur

No 22A, Block 2, Jalil Link Jalan Jalil
Jaya 2, Bukit Jalil 57000,
Kuala Lumpur, Malaysia
Phone: 60-3-8998-7877
Fax: 60-3-8998-7977
Email: malaysia@happy-science.org
Website: happyscience.org.my

Sao Paulo

Rua. Domingos de Morais 1154,
Vila Mariana, Sao Paulo SP
CEP 04010-100, Brazil
Phone: 55-11-5088-3800
Email: sp@happy-science.org
Website: happyscience.com.br

Kathmandu

Kathmandu Metropolitan City,
Ward No. 15, Ring Road, Kimdol,
Sitapaila Kathmandu, Nepal
Phone: 977-1-427-2931
Email: nepal@happy-science.org

Jundiai

Rua Congo, 447, Jd. Bonfiglioli
Jundiai-CEP, 13207-340, Brazil
Phone: 55-11-4587-5952
Email: jundiai@happy-science.org

Kampala

Plot 877 Rubaga Road, Kampala
P.O. Box 34130 Kampala, UGANDA
Phone: 256-79-4682-121
Email: uganda@happy-science.org

ABOUT HAPPINESS REALIZATION PARTY

The Happiness Realization Party (HRP) was founded in May 2009 by Master Ryuho Okawa as part of the Happy Science Group. HRP strives to improve the Japanese society, based on three basic political principles of "freedom, democracy, and faith," and let Japan promote individual and public happiness from Asia to the world as a leader nation.

1) Diplomacy and Security: Protecting Freedom, Democracy, and Faith of Japan and the World from China's Totalitarianism

Japan's current defense system is insufficient against China's expanding hegemony and the threat of North Korea's nuclear missiles. Japan, as the leader of Asia, must strengthen its defense power and promote strategic diplomacy together with the nations which share the values of freedom, democracy, and faith. Further, HRP aims to realize world peace under the leadership of Japan, the nation with the spirit of religious tolerance.

2) Economy: Early economic recovery through utilizing the "wisdom of the private sector"

Economy has been damaged severely by the novel coronavirus originated in China. Many companies have been forced into bankruptcy or out of business. What is needed for economic recovery now is not subsidies and regulations by the government, but policies which can utilize the "wisdom of the private sector."

For more information, visit en.hr-party.jp

HAPPY SCIENCE ACADEMY JUNIOR AND SENIOR HIGH SCHOOL

Happy Science Academy Junior and Senior High School is a boarding school founded with the goal of educating the future leaders of the world who can have a big vision, persevere, and take on new challenges.

Currently, there are two campuses in Japan; the Nasu Main Campus in Tochigi Prefecture, founded in 2010, and the Kansai Campus in Shiga Prefecture, founded in 2013.

Nasu Main Campus

Kansai Campus

HAPPY SCIENCE UNIVERSITY

THE FOUNDING SPIRIT AND THE GOAL OF EDUCATION

Based on the founding philosophy of the university, "Exploration of happiness and the creation of a new civilization," education, research and studies will be provided to help students acquire deep understanding grounded in religious belief and advanced expertise with the objectives of producing "great talents of virtue" who can contribute in a broad-ranging way to serving Japan and the international society.

FACULTIES

Faculty of human happiness

Students in this faculty will pursue liberal arts from various perspectives with a multidisciplinary approach, explore and envision an ideal state of human beings and society.

Faculty of successful management

This faculty aims to realize successful management that helps organizations to create value and wealth for society and to contribute to the happiness and the development of management and employees as well as society as a whole.

Faculty of future creation

Students in this faculty study subjects such as political science, journalism, performing arts and artistic expression, and explore and present new political and cultural models based on truth, goodness and beauty.

Faculty of future industry

This faculty aims to nurture engineers who can resolve various issues facing modern civilization from a technological standpoint and contribute to the creation of new industries of the future.

ABOUT HS PRESS

HS Press is an imprint of IRH Press Co., Ltd. IRH Press Co., Ltd., based in Tokyo, was founded in 1987 as a publishing division of Happy Science. IRH Press publishes religious and spiritual books, journals, magazines and also operates broadcast and film production enterprises. For more information, visit *okawabooks.com*.

Follow us on:

f Facebook: Okawa Books

▶ Youtube: Okawa Books

𝓟 Pinterest: Okawa Books

⬡ Instagram: OkawaBooks

🐦 Twitter: Okawa Books

g Goodreads: Ryuho Okawa

——— **NEWSLETTER** ———

To receive book related news, promotions and events, please subscribe to our newsletter below.

✆ eepurl.com/bsMeJj

——— **AUDIO / VISUAL MEDIA** ———

YOUTUBE   **PODCAST**

Introduction of Ryuho Okawa's titles; topics ranging from self-help, current affairs, spirituality, religion, and the universe.

Lightning Source UK Ltd.
Milton Keynes UK
UKHW010610030722
405253UK00002B/4